~~

# ALOHA

~~

# GREEN BANANAS

The Life and Times of a Hawaiian Tiki Bar

**BOOK 4**

# EVERETT PEACOCK

visit

# everett.peacock.com

No part of this publication may be reproduced, or stored in a retrieval system, or transmitted in any form or by any means, electronic, mechanical, photocopying, recording or otherwise, without written permission of the author. For information regarding permission, email to everett@peacock.com

paperback
ISBN-13: 978-1516921898
ISBN-10: 1516921895

ebook
ASIN: B0103LPZZK

v.1.2

Text copyright © 2015 by Everett Peacock.

# Other books by the Author

~~

## *The Life and Times of a Hawaiian Tiki Bar*

- book 1: The Parrot Talks In Chocolate
- book 2: In the Middle of the Third Planet's Most Wonderful of Oceans
- book 3: Tiwaka Goes to Waikiki
- book 4: Green Bananas

~~

## Death by Facebook

~~

## Escaping the Magnificent

~~

## Escape from Hanalei

~~

## The Galactics

~~

## A Paradise of One

~~~

don't disregard your **dreams**,

they just might be your only

hope

~~~

# PREFACE

The adventure begun in 2009 has yet another chapter now.

Tiwaka's Tiki Bar & Grill. One of those places I would hang out at every evening, if I could. However, that day is only possible within the confines of this series of four books.

Prior to this particular book over 60,000 copies have been distributed to a world thirsty for tropical escapism served with a heaping helping of magical realism.

Maui, the setting for all four books, is indeed a special place. It has its problems, like most places only bordering on perfection, but they are easy to accommodate, or ignore.

For instance, we are constantly threatened with tropical storms and hurricanes in the summer, but there has never been a direct hit on the island since records or memories began. As Matthew Peacock likes to say, "Maui's like the boy that cried storm" We are fortunate that way.

Maui is also a place of sometimes conflicting ideologies, some old, some new, all of them passionately defended. It's an interesting showcase of competing visions for the future, some of which quite literally play with fire.

Yet, as Michael Peacock reminded me once, "What if cavemen didn't play with fire?" Good point.

Everett Peacock  
August 26, 2015  
Kula, Maui, Hawaii

~~
Dedicated to

... you

~~

# TIWAKA'S TIKI BAR & GRILL
## GRAND OPENING OF THE LAHAINA FRANCHISE

### MAUI, THE HAWAIIAN ISLANDS

She was dressed to do me harm.

Silk seemed to drape her shoulders. Yet, as she moved closer I could see she wore only a standard surfer tee just above some après-beach shorts. It was *her* that moved as silk, just underneath that most fortunate cotton.

No one else in the packed ocean side bar seemed to notice the new arrival. When her eyes swung through the crowd, calculating, searching, and found mine, I could tell that she knew I had noticed.

Her subtle smile captured my breath, squeezing it around my heart with a practiced caress. Lightly brushing long dark brown curls away from her arched, inquisitive eyebrow focused my attention, evaporating the crowd and the bar noise. Her pushing those full lips just far enough out so that they would slowly retreat back onto themselves, inviting me to follow, managed to stop all measures of time. Right before I fell completely off my bar stool I caught myself stepping all over the approaching waitress.

"Hey big guy," she said with more patience than I deserved. Turning her head to follow my stare, she whistled lightly to herself.

"Wow... she's back." She slid past me, uncaring that she had pushed her breasts right into my shoulders. Placing her order for the kitchen, she turned back to me, whispering from behind my ear. "She's not what you think."

Perching myself back up on my bar stool I turned to the waitress. Her eyes were averted for just a moment but found mine after some hesitation. She had a brief wash of sadness in her expression, then looked back over to the woman, whispering.

"I don't think you're her type." It took her several seconds before she broke her stare and looked back at me, flashing a quick unauthentic smile.

My fascination was broken with the perceived insult. I frowned for the moment it took me to respond, then shook it off.

"Ah..." turning to her directly and smiling my own manufactured smile. "You mean the incredibly desirous, witty and charming, well-traveled type?"

Her laugh was brief and she seemed to weigh her answer. I could hear her breath letting out slowly, as if now resigned to tell me.

"No," she let her eyes hold mine for the moment it took for me to understand she was serious, then quickly looked down to her tray. "Watch her closely. That should be no problem," she practically scolded me. And never looked up again. "Tell me what you see, big guy. I'm here til closing."

With that she hefted her tray full of rainbow-colored fruit drinks and spiced fish, flexed the minimum number of muscles to do so, and walked into the crowd. I turned back to look for the girl in the silk body.

She was still moving in my direction.

A moment later, now standing inches away from me, was the most beautiful woman who surely had ever existed.  Silk.  Sexy.

Intoxicating.

She was indeed dressed to do me harm.  When her hand finally touched my arm, I felt the sweet thorns of addiction anchoring permanently into my soul.

~~~

"How's my brother doing?" I asked while pouring some Ocean Vodka into an already opened coconut.

"He's acting like he hasn't seen a female in years," the waitress said, politely trying to push Tiwaka a few inches off to the side, away from her tray.

"Year and a half," I corrected.  "Did he make a pass at you, Alana?"

"No, no.  He's acting all gentleman like," Alana placed two Coco Loco Moco drinks in their special holders on her tray.  Round coconuts tend to fall from unsupported serving trays.  She leaned in a bit closer.  "Was he in prison?"

Before I could answer, she turned and whispered to the parrot.

"I always wanted to get me a guy right out of prison."  She giggled uncontrollably, forcing Tiwaka to take two measured steps backward.

"No prison, wild child." I turned to put the Ocean Vodka back and grab a bottle of local rum. "Probably worse."

Alana turned toward the crowd, her tray now impossibly full. "I'll be back for the rest of *that story*." She moved into the throngs of dancers, posers and fascinated tourists, swinging her hips as much to navigate as to entice any gawkers.

Tiwaka's Tiki Bar & Grill ~ Lahaina, was our newest expansion and so far our most popular. Waikiki was a close second, but my heart would always be with our still open, but rarely visited jungle original about a two-hour drive from here. Ma and Pa kept the place open for their friends and those lucky few who managed to stumble across the place. Ha'iku still gathered a bit more magic than other communities.

This was our first week and the curious were filling the place. The stories of some kind of mystic parrot (actually a Macaw) who predicted the future and understood the past, had preceded the first nail of construction. Tours were even setup by some enterprising Honolulu guys bringing the hedonistic Waikiki crowd to Lahaina. Via cruise ships.

Yes, business was brisk and scary profitable.

The local bars were worried at first. Mick Fleetwood had wandered in during lunch, probably afraid of some serious competition for his own rocking joint only a block away, but when he didn't see a drum set, he smiled, nodded toward the bar and left.

Cheeseburger in Paradise had sent some spies, but we got them deeply involved with some free Coco Loco Moco's and when the taxi picked them up, Tiwaka slipped a feather behind each of their ears. Well, I helped a little with that.

The message was well received.

A compromise was reached. They wouldn't sell coconut drinks and we wouldn't sell cheeseburgers.

We even had an offer from the owner of the nearby island of Lana'i to build a Tiwaka's at a new harbor he was using to create sailing's best America's Cup team. That was a big maybe at the moment. There was only one parrot and one bartender who could talk to the bird. I was already spread thin between three bars, surfing Unknowns as much as possible and chasing baby Kiawe around. Add Sandy's incredible magnetism to that mix and it was a wonder I could tell time, much less manage it at all.

Tonight was super-busy. One of the bar backs had broken an arm surfing the shallows at Honolua Bay. No one was surprised, but I was still short one very valuable set of hands.

The parrot was having to help out a bit. I asked Tiwaka to count heads since I thought we might be close to the Lahaina Fire Department maximum. Every time I looked to him for an answer he looked away. OK - we must be close. Really close.

I delivered three Luau Bombs to the surf crew at the end of the bar and just above their sun-bleached hair could easily see Alana practically running back to her station.

"OK," she breathlessly asked. "What's worse than prison?"

"It's a long story, you got time for that?"

"No," Alana agreed, looking back at a packed bar. "Give me the twenty-second version plus four Blink 182's, an Einstein and two vodka tonics, house."

I began mixing and pouring as Tiwaka began one of his long marches down the bar.  Everyone saw him coming, knew the routine and covered their drinks.  The crazy bird had a new, bad habit.  He would pluck an ice cube from an unguarded glass, throw it up into the air, flap his great wings enough to ruffle everyone's hair, and catch the tumbling cube in his beak.  Then whistle impossibly loud just as he crushed it into a hundred shards.  Nice circus trick.  Messy show.

"He's actually my half-brother," I started.  "Mom's side.  Never lived on the island for long.  Crazy smart, went to college early and then to NASA.  He's just been up on the space station for eighteen months, with only himself at best or a couple of hairy Russians at worse, the entire time."

Alana looked at me as if I were making it all up.

"Seriously," I tried to add some manufactured authenticity to the story, even if it were already entirely true.  "The last eight months it was just him and whatever supply rockets they could send up.  The Russians and us don't play nice together anymore, you know.  He was stranded, basically.  Finally, Space X sent a replacement crew up and Hudson got placed on immediate leave.  Psychological leave actually.  Doctors said he needed some serious ground time, and well... here he is, in the family bar, on a Saturday night, in Lahaina!"

Alana was staring at me, her mouth slightly open, until Tiwaka started whistling with one of the surfer guy's ice cubes in his beak.  She glanced at the bird, back to me and nodded acknowledgment.  Her face had a tinge of sadness.  I could see it bubbling up slightly beneath her perfect tan and cute dimples.

"That was more like forty-five seconds," she said softly. I placed the last drink into the last open space on her tray. "Poor guy," she said under her breath, turning back into the crowd.

~~~

"Hudson," I said, holding out my hand. I think she had said her name but the bar was so noisy I couldn't catch it. I leaned over closer, feeling her long curls against my forehead. She was purposely speaking softly.

"I saw you watching me," she said.

"Me and every other guy in here tonight," I admitted.

"No. They're not."

"What? You're quite…"

She pulled back before I could finish my compliment, but her smile contained enough promise to thwart any disappointment I might feel knocking on the door of my confidence. Holding up two fingers, in the old peace symbol salute, she headed toward the main bar.

I reached for, and found behind me, the melted ice cubes that had once decorated some kind of pineapple virgin. The last of its coolness was vaporizing right at my lips as the hot Lahaina evening took its toll. The glass was warm and no comfort at all to my sweaty palms. The top of my jeans legs would have to do.

She had disappeared into the crowd, as was probably appropriate. Beautiful women had never paid me much attention, unless I held a door for them, or saved their life, and then only for about as long as this one had.

It never hurt.

That's OK. I was in paradise now, literally. Human paradise. Only three hours ago I had just finished spending ten hours inside a Boeing 777 with its highly scrubbed air conditioning, and before that three days in a NASA medical unit breathing the chilled and almost imperceptible fumes of whatever chemicals they like to disinfect the place with. Just before that it had been forty-three minutes in a rapid descent from Earth orbit, sucking up an entire bottle of bland, tasteless oxygen. And, for the previous eighteen months to that wild ride, I had been floating above this paradise in an enclosed self-sustaining space station where we recycled our air, our urine and our hopes.

I had not actually touched another human being for the entire time. On the space station, no one touched my hand, ever. We shook hands with the new arrivals, those departing, and never again had any occasion to touch anyone. It was weird, but OK, in a strange, professional way. But, then no one was expected to live like that for eighteen months.

I remember, upon my return, a nurse reaching for and pulling my arm toward her for a blood pressure measurement. It was the most intimate thing anyone had shared with me in a very long time. She was the exception. She just didn't know it.

The doctors had gotten a little personal with me, but only to the extent that a robot would if it was to scan you for cancer or infection, spit out a report and reboot itself before the next patient.

Here... here was a different universe altogether.

Here, in this bar, I can smell the humanity and it is captivating and wonderful, and repulsive at the same time. The crowd is humid, more so than the tropical air, already thick with distant night-blooming flowers and sea air. These people are fascinating, all fellow Earthlings that amazingly enough are all related to me. Remote perspectives found in spaceflight taught me that. We're all one tribe, stuck out in the middle of nowhere.

I watch every person I can in the bar. They move in fluid patterns around the room. Their bodies pulse just under the rhythm of the music they dance to. Their voices resonate with my skin, my very bones. Some of them are repulsive, others intoxicating but they are all emanating scents from their skin, their hair, and their clothes. Even their drinks are wildly fragrant.

A group of men move from the dance floor back to their tables. I think they smell like horses, not unpleasant but strong and pungent as freshly washed horses might smell. Another man, dressed impeccably with gold chains around his wrist, an open shirt and damp hair, wafts by. Currents of expensive body wash fumes follow closely.

The waitress I had talked to earlier, glances at me for just a moment and quickly looks away as she places several highly decorated drinks on a table close by. The ripeness of sweet fruit is unmistakable, mixing with the strong alcohol content my brother is famous for, and the smell of the sea just outside.

The women, though... some of the women are irresistible. The few, not over doused in fake aromas that infuriate my nose, the ones that sport a light sheen from dancing - they capture my attention. The glistening of light on their skin decorates their necks and the wonderful valleys that fall just below. The fewer still that happen to walk closely past me, glance up to catch my eye, then demurely move along, leave me famished. I try to take as deep of a breath as I can, to capture their scent, without appearing obvious, or strange.

I catch myself, for a moment, entertaining that strange worry.

In space you're never self-conscious. There is no one else around. At least not for most of my stay, there wasn't. You don't have to shave, bathe daily or even suppress your burps. You can be alone with your thoughts, and actually think. Think about things dozens and dozens of steps long, imagining variations that might be favored if this, then or that.

It was, I eventually discovered, only self-indulgent behavior, nothing more glorious than that.

Maybe that's why I signed up in the first place. I had lusted for such solitary time. Space promised plenty of it. But, I had to keep my obsession a secret. NASA wanted the most well-adjusted people possible. What they got were a few smart people who could fake it. I worked hard to make it happen, and it did. I finally got my precious solitary universe, away from the overwhelming noise of... everything. The world was a chaotic scream of desperation. I couldn't fix it. So, I ran away to space. To be solitary, to be safe.

But, I was wrong. Solitary confinement sucks. Space sucks. The lack of noise, the absence of predictable chaos and the missing imperfections of society, made it so impossibly artificial.

Artificial. I couldn't recycle that. The view was spectacular, the job was important, I guess, but it was lacking.

Lacking this... human paradise.

Just as I put my glass back on the table behind me and turned around I saw her again, across the bar. I noticed her appear almost as a mist from within the crowd, moving her silk limbs on bare feet, watching me as she approached with two tall glasses of something green and pink.

Yes, I had been gone too long. Far too long.

She walked right up to me, close. Too close for strangers. I looked down just to see how damn close she was standing.

Deliciously close.

Her beautiful self was standing between my open knees. There it was, I suddenly noticed, my heart was racing. The first drop of sweat on my brow began to move.

She was sending me a message and I wasn't too space-stupid to not see it. Rising between us, slowly and deliberately, was ...her hand holding that impossibly colored green and pink drink in a tall... a very tall, glass. Her own glass was right next to it, and as I took mine from her fingers, she tapped her glass to mine.

"Cheers," I said softly, in case my voice broke with nervousness. It came out sounding like a whisper.

She nodded and let her smile widen. "Tatiana," she announced. "And, you are Hudson, I believe."

"Tatiana," I repeated, feeling my grin a bit extreme but unwilling to reign it in. "Ta-ti-ana," I said to myself. How beautiful is that?

We each drank deeply from our identical glasses. I was staring at her throat, she into my eyes. When I looked up I saw admiration; not in me of course, but in the fact that I had noticed. She moved in closer, touching my left thigh with her hip.

"I think we should dance," her eyes invited. Her hand insisted.

I stood, feeling the alcohol in the green part of the drink descend on its own, stinging my throat, but in that old comfortable way that happened only while on the ground. I didn't have to force it down, like I did in space. It was being pulled down. That was comforting.

Super comforting.

Everything was so directional here, what with the steady pull below my feet. I stepped toward her, relishing the slight resistance I felt with my feet.

Gravity. Its return was a bit overwhelming, but rapidly becoming familiar again. I was quickly enjoying the fact that I didn't have to bounce off walls in zero gravity anymore. Taking Tatiana's hand after we finished the drinks, I looked forward to moving against her and not bouncing away.

The music was deep and rhythmic. Perfectly loud. I moved in closer and watched her writhe as my mirror image, moving with me, in to my out, out to my in.

We throbbed with the crowd, our very blood pulsing to the drum beat, our muscles flexing in perfect timing to the rhythm. Everyone around me was happy, swirling in the same whirlpool of humanity.

Tatiana pulled me close as the music slowed. Her skin against mine felt like that of a wild animal. I felt lips on my ear, whispering, promising there would be two wild animals.

I could smell her, of course. Somewhere between a floral and high mountain pasture scent that I'm quite sure existed nowhere else on Earth. Or above Earth.

# KA'ANAPALI BEACH HOTEL

Tiwaka has no respect for late mornings in bed. Early bird, the worm - that's surely his problem. Except, this morning it's my problem.

I had good reason to stay in bed after being short-handed at the bar. However, my main reason was far more immediate. Sandy was wrapped around my sleepy body, arms and legs intertwined in some kind of circus hug, while baby Kiawe slept quietly in his little outrigger canoe-bed.

The parrot, though, was pacing back and forth between the sunlit window and the black out curtain. His feathered butt was sticking out into the room, wiggling every time I heard a mynah bird squawk. I could only imagine the funny faces those birds were making at Tiwaka, teasing him about being stuck inside the "cage with no bars", or *windows* as the humans knew them.

I had plans to wake up Sandy in our favorite way, but with Tiwaka loose in the room I didn't want a repeat of him perched on my back yelling "Hana Hou". That had only been funny the first time.

Untangling myself from Sandy was going to be my first challenge. We were facing each other, her head turned toward the ceiling and a lone curl moving in the light breeze from her open mouth. Sliding my right arm from in between her left arm and her waist must have tickled her a little and she immediately threw her thigh atop my waist. Her head rolled toward me, putting her neck up against the tip of my nose.

Baby Kiawe burped in his sleep. At least I think it was a burp. It probably wasn't.

I was still stuck.

Tiwaka was actively irritating the mynah birds now. From the sound of it there must be a dozen on so on our small lanai just outside the window. That noise alone would wake everyone in a half dozen rooms either side of ours. Or not.

Sandy didn't budge. So, I gently slid my right arm back so that I could push her thigh off my hip and I rotated left. I was making good progress keeping her asleep, but less keeping myself completely focused on escape. The more her soft skin was sliding against mine, the more I was visualizing Tiwaka on my back again.

As I rotated left to get out from under her, Sandy rolled again, this time pinning me completely underneath her.

"Good morning," she whispered. "Going somewhere?"

I wanted to answer but kisses on my neck always paralyze my vocal chords.

"Just… trying to… get the bird…" I managed to squeak out only a few syllables at a time between kisses. The opportunity to secure the bird before things got rolling was fading in inverse proportion to my heart rate.

"Tiwaka is loose…" I finally said.

Sandy stopped kissing me for a second. She propped herself up on her hands, her long hair still reaching my chest, and looked over at the curtain.

In a second she had leaped off the bed, grabbed the bird and locked him in the bathroom. Taking only a second or three to glance at her sleeping baby, she seductively climbed back up onto the bed.

"Like I was saying," as she moved in closer. "Good morning."

~~~

Breakfast at the Ka'anapali Beach Hotel is one of my favorite pleasures in a life full of pleasures. The original hotel, the first to be built on Maui's best and most spectacular stretch of sand, had avoided remodeling for decades. Other hotels and resorts had popped up on either side of the sprawling, coconut-palm graced lawns. Each had their own "Disney-esque" swimming pool which initially had harmed the KBH. Kids, and their protective parents, preferred an action filled pool to an unpredictable ocean. Even if that ocean was damn near pristine.

But, wait long enough and your hesitation opens the door to Retro fashion and a desire for the old days. Now, the tiny pool didn't distract from the palatial grounds, the small Tiki bar suited one's thirst just fine and the friendly staff all knew each other so well that you smiled when you saw them laughing together.

At the Ka'anapali Beach Hotel you relished in the feeling that your vacation in Hawaii was in no danger of being "over-produced".

This is a hotel you can actually relax at. As long as you don't have a parrot in your room irritating the Mynahs just outside your window, you'll find it magical.

# GREEN BANANAS

Opening week at Tiwaka's Tiki Bar & Grill had been a resounding success. Picking January to open had been a great idea, plenty of tourists and our famously dry and sunny weather here on the planet's most accommodating island.

But, there were risks associated with January.

The days were shorter, and therefore the nights were longer. It wasn't an extreme dichotomy like you would find in Toronto or Anchorage, but that three and a half hour difference in daylight had a distinct effect on the local labor force.

Tropical folks didn't mind working when the sun was up, but watch out when it went down, or even got close to that shimmering horizon. It was like a heavy gravitational syrup moved into their veins. Things slowed down. Way down. Less productivity.

Added to this was the fact that January was the month we received our seasonal blessings from the north. Big waves. Every young man and woman who could swim, hold their breath for a full two minutes underwater when necessary and had the courage to do so were challenging their friends, themselves and nature itself. God bless 'em, but that cut into productivity as well.

Finally, and most folks would find this observation ludicrous, but it could get *cold* here. Yes, I said that nasty four letter word. That particular four letter word, of all the four letter words in English that were commonly heard in Lahaina, that was rarely uttered. C.O.L.D.

The same storm that would soon slam into the Canadian west coast bearing several feet of snow had a wispy little tail that had crossed the channel between Molokai and Honolulu during the night and continued across Maui at dawn. People were seen physically shaking all over town. It was so cold....

HOW COLD WAS IT?

It was so cold I would have worn two pairs of socks if I owned more than one.

Fortunately, I was keeping warmer than most since I was hauling into the bar one of Pa's record setting Haiku banana stalks. It had to be over a hundred pounds. Of course it was heavier than it should have been....Tiwaka was perched on the top as I struggled to get it hung on the hook next to the vodka.

Tiwaka squawked and ducked under the door jam, missing disaster by an inch. Instead of apologizing I thanked him for alerting me to lower the bananas enough to get through the door. It took him an entire day to catch the irony.

"Bananas!"

Several of the morning cleaning crew dropped their brooms and mops and ran over. Quickly, I heard a collective sigh as they stopped and turned back to their work.

"Green bananas," I heard them moan. Their words sounded so sad. Disappointment ran thick among them.

I concentrated on the last ten feet toward the "banana pincher" my brother had invented before he had fled to university. Ropes and hooks were so old school. Now, all I had to do was slide a couple of inches of the stalk up into this open tube-inside-of-a-tube. Backwards facing teeth let me slide the stem deeper. As soon as I let gravity try and pull the bananas down, those teeth took hold. That motion was leveraged by the rotation of those teeth on a swivel which swung the 'jaws' holding the teeth to slant inward, effectively pinning the stem with as much force as its weight contributed. Brilliant.

After securing the heavy stalk I activated the electric winch to lift them up to about one foot above the bar surface.

Yeah, we did this often. In fact, the last two Tiwaka franchises had this winch feature designed in from construction day.

I had a lot of banana sap on my hands. As I washed up I glanced up to the cleaning crew. They were all staring at me, holding their brooms and mops like crutches.

"What's wrong?" I asked. I turned off the water.

One of the younger of the crew looked at the others, quickly back to me and then spoke up.

"They're green."

I nodded. Of course they were.

"Yeah. Bananas..." I looked a bit closer at their faces. It looked as if I had brought soured ice cream. "Don't worry, they'll be ripe soon."

The cleaning crew nodded knowingly and went back to work. The younger one stood still and watched his co-workers get busy. He shook his head and glanced at me before looking down at the floor.

I could hear him whisper to himself.

"They're not ripe now."

These bananas were magnificent, even in their greenness. They had lost their triangular look and had begun to round themselves. Each hand must have had twenty bananas waving, trying to impress the other hands just above.

"Look," I had to add. "Isn't this an awesome manifestation of vegetative art." The room got quieter. "Seriously, the banana plant that made this... I mean, look at this. It's five times heavier than the mother it came from." I looked around at several confused faces. "Nowhere else in nature does this happen. Animal or plant."

I wasn't convincing them. The bananas were green. They couldn't be eaten. Everyone would have to wait. At least a week.

Maybe two.

~~~

That evening, as the regulars wandered in early to get their seats at the bar, I noticed the old cowboy frowning. He had been showing up nightly for several days, always sitting at the end of the bar. Just where I had hung the green bananas.

Most folks thought the stalk of fruit was a nice tropical touch. Something you didn't see in the other Lahaina bars, something that had a better chance of putting you in the desired state of mind.

Finally, I had to ask.

"What's up?" I quickly pushed another Aloha Lager in his direction. "Why the sour face?"

When he looked up at me I could see that he might actually be older than I had first imagined. Quite a bit older.

"Green bananas," he pouted, pointing at the stalk only an arm's length away.

I shook my head a little. Another complaint! What was it with everyone and my not-yet-ripe bananas? I turned to admire them.

"They'll be ready in a week or two."

Looking back to the old cowboy I could tell he wasn't finding my answer satisfactory. Years of experience working behind the bar had taught me, usually the hard way, that people's emotions were often stronger than their ability to express them. Perhaps he was just having a little trouble telling me what could possibly be wrong with green bananas.

"Tell you what," I offered. "I'll save you the first ones that ripen. We can make you a custom Coco Loco Moco smoothie that is to die for…"

Immediately, I regretted my choice of words. I had never liked "to die for" but I had just heard some teenagers use it and thought I might try it to soften the old man's apparent disappointment. It didn't work.

"Don't bother, kiddo," he grumbled.

I turned away.

There was nothing I could do here. The waitress station had some action. As I filled the few orders filtering in I couldn't get the old cowboy's issue out of my mind.

As with all mysteries, I knew a consult with Tiwaka would probably shine some light on a solution. The parrot would know. Looking back down the bar at my green bananas I notice the old cowboy had disappeared.

# LEARNING TO FLY RAINBOWS

Eventually, even on small islands in the middle of the ocean, influenza shows up. Not the bad stuff mind you, but just enough to remind you that paradise is a click or two below absolutely perfect.

I was in the middle of my first bad cold in a decade and trying real hard to remember if it was really supposed to be this uncomfortable. Is this stuff survivable, I wondered, with some concern? Sandy assured me it was, as she wrapped me a warm blanket and propped me up in the cliff-side hammock we often shared. The trade winds had disappeared for a few days and with a warm sun, filtered nicely between small ocean clouds, it did indeed feel good to be out of bed and in the world again. The shade from the guava trees holding up my hammock kept the temperature on the cool side of warm. It had been a brilliant idea to leave Lahaina and recuperate at our home in the jungle.

"Honey ..." she said it so sweetly I had to check quickly that I had not already died and was hearing angels whisper to me.

"Oh," I focused back to reality. "Yes, thank you."

She looked at me quizzically, "Are you going to be alright out here?" Her hand went to my forehead for the twentieth time that morning. I wondered if her hand might be capable of sucking the heat from my skin or it was simply depositing more by constantly touching me. "You still feel a little hot. The ibuprofen should kick in any minute now."

I smiled as best I could, but that upset the fragile balance between gravity and the copious amount of fluids in my sinuses and I had to quickly bring a tissue up to my nose.

"OK," she said. "So you've got your phone there, and your water bottle and a book," she paused and knelt down next to me. "But, I suggest you take a nice nap." Her eyes were deeper than I knew I would ever be able to swim out of. "Will you, please?"

"Yeah baby, no worries, I'm half way there now." Another smile was stopped dead in its tracks by the incredible effort it took.

Sandy stood up, put her hands on her hips and looked at me for a long moment. I might be sick, half dead and full of snot, but I still could appreciate a Tahitian beauty when I saw one that close. Her legs were bronzed and strong, her shorts tied around her small waist with rope and her belly button still moved together with her breath.

For the first time ever, since we had met I felt the urge to grab her and pull her to me but didn't have the physical power to do so. A burst of sun came flying out from behind the cloud it had hidden so well behind and forced my eyes shut. It was just as well, I needed to change my focus.

"Sweet dreams baby," Sandy whispered as she turned and walked back down the grassy trail to the Ma and Pa's bar.

I think I said "Aloha" but I may have only thought I said it, as my eyes felt incredibly good remaining shut.

The sun stirred a small breeze within the cane fields behind the hammock toward Haleakala, which did me the great favor of rustling my hair and cooling my fever a little. That felt delicious! Do it again, I thought. This time, the breeze, small and delicate came at me from the sea cliff, twirled between my bare toes and slid up to my face with a most subtle kiss. I opened my mouth slightly to inhale as much of her as I could ...

*I blinked a little at the sun again but noticed now the shade came from majestic coconut palms hovering over a smoothly washed sand that my toes were enjoying sinking into. I felt a lot better suddenly and looked out to the ocean as perfect head high glassy waves peeled on either side of a small channel opening in the reef. No one was in the water, and I noticed then that there were no footprints in the sand either. Stopping for a moment and looking behind me I saw there were no footprints there either.*

I must have fallen immediately into a dream, at least I think I must have. My sleep was fitful with my clogged up nose forcing me awake, often. As I blew into the tissues I noticed that I remembered my dream, heck I was still half asleep, but half enough awake to realize what was going on.

Gently I laid my head back down, breathed a little deeply. Once, twice and then let my mind go back to continue the story ...

*The beach had a gentle slope down into a reef-protected lagoon that glistened in the brilliant tropical light. Schools of small silver fish jumped up and away from larger ones, little crabs the size of a small coin moved in and out of holes in the sand, piling pebbles around the edges and taking a moment to look at me before going back to work.*

*I noticed the surf again, it was indeed perfect. Having no particular place to go, I sat down in a gently waving shadow of a large frond above me and watched the show. Turtles played in the channel* that cut through the reef, often diving like a whale might and showing off their proud short tales and flipper feet.

Looking to my left, the coastline wove itself in and out of a couple of small coves before disappearing behind a large sandy point. The coconut trees were so tightly packed on this point it looked like they had all raced up to the ocean's edge and then stopped all at once when they saw the water.

Behind all of them were a series of green mountains, stubby and fading to a point in the distance. I got the feeling that this island ended somewhere close by or turned a corner there.

Looking to my right I saw a miles long coastline holding at arms distance a white foaming line of surf tracing the beaches all the way to where the island turned again, in the far distance. Short headlands, graced in green, held this scene at its feet, but no tall mountains guided them. Their beauty was their own.

My eyes drifted back to the sound of peeling waves, throwing light off their smooth glistening surfaces in ways I had not seen a painter reproduce yet. I had never even seen photos capture this quite as well. In fact, the more I looked at the show the more I wondered if it might be a unique view one gets from being present, from being here.

What could possibly capture all of this? The soft sand that cradled me, my bare feet sinking into the cool colorful grains, the warming sun on my skin and the soft sounds of palm fronds playing in the background. All while my eyes fascinated me with a tropical scene that almost made me laugh at its absolute beauty.

The horizon, where the two best shades of blue met, was bare and pure, only patches of white birds feeding on leftovers from some underwater drama I couldn't see. No one was to be seen, no evidence that anyone might have ever been here ...

"Tasty waves this morning."

I turned quickly to my left. He looked at me and smiled and then looked back out to the surf, sitting only three feet away from me.

"Looks like it has the perfect amount of west in it, don't you think?" He looked back at me, nodding his head almost imperceptibly.

I had to break my stare and blink and finally found my manners.

"Yeah," I managed to mutter. Where did this guy show up from? Again, I noticed no footprints, anywhere. "It does look pretty awesome out there."

I looked closely at this guy, quite a bit older than me, actually I would have to say he was elderly. Yet, he looked quite fit, healthy and yet, as I studied him further, he appeared to be really old! If I could imagine a 100-year-old surfer this might be him!

He turned to look at me again, and I caught his eye. My god! He looked startling familiar. It was his eyes that made the connection, but before I could say anything he asked,

"Are you going out?"

I broke his gaze, disturbing as it was and looked back out to the surf. Another long left was peeling itself lazily across the reef.

"I ... I don't have a board ..."

Turning back to him, I saw him looking down between us. I looked down too and saw a surfboard on its back between us in the sand.

*Dreams have a way of skipping ahead to the important parts, and leaving out all those distracting details we are bound to in reality. Things, or people, suddenly appearing was never as shocking as it would have been say back at the bar. Here, now, was my old favorite board from so many years ago! Six foot eight inches long, thick, too thick to duck dive, and wide. The tri-fin had an experimental scoop fin in the middle and there just below the rainbow colors airbrushed near the nose were the words "Dinosaur Beach"*

My nose woke me up, again. Its capacity to hold copious amounts of liquid had been breached. My hand went to my side for more tissue as I turned gently toward Sandy's table. I felt for the box but had to open my eyes to find it on the edge.

This dream, I noticed as I blew hard and long, was drawing me like a loose chocolate rolling on the bar for Tiwaka. Almost. I wasn't as frantic as Tiwaka would be. But, I was just as captivated. That beach! I remember it well, one of the secret gems in Hawaii. Known, but really hidden and practically ignored. My good friend from those days, Billy Bingle, and I used to surf there all the time. Lived on that very beach, laughed at our incredible good fortune and relished in the notion, the one we kept to ourselves, that these days might very well be our best.

Sometimes, for some fortunate souls, you realize your best days while you are in them. For us, it was like a secret blessing from God or the Universe or Whomever. We didn't know why us, but we figured it might have something to do with us being aware. Aware and appreciative.

One night, after a third perfect surf session of the day, reef lobster for dinner and several Australian beers, Billy and I took a walk down the darkened beach to clear our heads.  The Milky Way was so bright we thought it first to be high clouds in the pure dark tropical canopy.  Billy was my neighbor, living next door about as simply as I was.  He was one of those rare souls that sees the bright side of most things.  But, when he was standing in the midst of perfection he had to put on sunglasses – the present was so bright.  Neither of us paid much attention to the future in those days.

"Yo, dude, can you believe today?" I asked, my full party-mode dialect rising to the surface.

"Oh, yeah!" Billy said.  "This is so awesome!"

Yes, it's true.  We really did talk like this and the funny thing is that we weren't pretending or posing.  Our language was spot on.

Billy and I had both done a little surf traveling over the days.  Bali, Australia – both coasts, California – north and south, France, even Costa Rica.  Tahiti.  Florida, North Carolina.  The offshore islands of Georgia.  Various Caribbean secret spots.  Yet, where did we live?  Hawaii, of course.  The best surf, the best weather, the best lifestyle, the ultimate in all things we found important at the time was here.

"Dude, you know …" I said, waxing eloquent.  "This is the best beach.  The best."

Billy was silent for a moment as he considered that.  I did as well, and now that I think about it, I feel we might very well have been sharing the same thought at that moment.

"Yeah," Billy said after a moment.  "We do have the best surf, sometimes.  Like today."

Other places had great surf too, though. So, that wasn't it altogether.

"No doubt," I added. "We've got tasty lobsters hiding in the reef caves we surf over! Isn't that cool?"

Billy was nodding his head yes in the starlit glow from above us. "Yeah, I know!" He looked over at me briefly, caught my eye, and turned back to look out at the white foam of a wave painting a glow from right to left.

"There's better surf, sometimes, in other places," I said. "But, we've got electricity, and cars, and jobs - airline jobs I know - perfect for us, but they're still jobs. And, we've got MTV on cable, and all the food we can afford, and perfect weather, and no snakes, or poison ivy, or war, or gangs or any of that shit!"

"Unreal!" Billy exclaimed. "None of that shit! It's so… good!"

We walked another few meters down the beach, breathing in the offshore flow of air that was bringing the plumeria and night blooming jasmine fragrances down to the sea.

"All the other great beaches, they have some kind of problem," Billy added.

"Yeah," I nodded in the darkness. "We've got no crowds, no sea snakes, no urchins, no hungry sharks. We've got no crowds!"

"You know what?" Billy asked.

"What?"

"This is the best beach on Earth!" He stopped in his tracks at the magnitude of that pronouncement. I did as well.

"Awesome! Yes! It's the best on Earth!" I yelled at the top of my voice. Naturally, only Billy heard me. We were in the midst of desolate perfection.

We both heard the crack of a bigger wave breaking over the reef, and we turned and watch another, yes!, another amazingly beautiful wave peel itself unridden in the star shine.

"You know," I began letting my mind wander as it tends to do when I am right. "There's no surf on the sun, or Mercury or Venus, at least nothing we can ride. The moon, nada. Mars' oceans dried up a long time ago, Jupiter and Saturn, too cold for wetsuits even. And, those other outer planet's are frozen." I held my hands up into the sky as if I might embrace the massive astronomical facts I was describing. "It's the best beach in the entire Solar System dude!" I added. We both were laughing - it was true. No, really, it was. Considering MTV it had to be true.

Billy looked at me and smiled. I could see him grinning widely. He put out his hand.

"To the only two lucky guys standing in front of perfect surf on the Solar System's best beach!" He grasped my hand firmly. I knew he was right. These were indeed our best days, and I think we both knew it at that moment. We knew it very, very ... very well.

*There I was again, on that same beach, sitting in the warm sand. The old guy I had just met was walking back out of the water, holding my board. The sun was shining on the water sheeting from his old but taunt skin. His muscles looked thin but strong.*

"Ah, you're back!" he said. Walking back over he gently put my board back between us. "Tasty waves indeed," he added, running his hands through his wet, white hair.

"How long ... how long was I gone?"

He laughed a little, kicked some sand toward a scurrying crab several feet away and nodded to himself. I had seen that nod before, as a kid, when an adult would ignore some silly question I had asked.

"I caught the best wave I've had in a very, very long time," he smiled, pointing out to the where the reef was producing epic left barrels just big enough to let a surfer crouch inside with little effort.

I let my question go unanswered.

My hammock moved up and down a bit as the guava trees took a hold of some wind off the mountain. My dream paused as I turned a little to get more comfortable, but I kept my eyes shut, hoping to re-enter my story. Before I did, though, I caught a nice whiff of plumeria before drifting off again ...

"Smell that?" The old guy asked, turning to look behind us, toward the coconut groves. "Plumeria!" He laughed out loud. "Don't get that on the beach very often do you?"

I did smell it, of course. I had brought it with me, into this dream. I suppose I had also brought the perfect surf, the warm sunshine seeping into my skin and even my old favorite surfboard. This stretch of coastline was my former home, where Billy Bingle and I had discovered the best beach in the solar system. I knew every detail here implicitly and was actually a little proud that I had been able to reproduce it so well.

*I let his question go unanswered.*

*"You know," I began. "I've been here before, this beach." I looked around again, just to make sure. Several turtles were cruising just off the sand in the rock-less shallows so clear it looked as if they might really be flying low off the ground.*

*"I know this scene about as well as I know most anything," I continued. "Everything about this dream of mine makes sense... except you." I turned to look at the old man. He was already watching me intently, his eyes peering into me as if they might extract some treasure.*

*He nodded and looked out to the surf again. "Yeah, I know what you mean, it's just like we left it, isn't it? Maybe even better?"*

*A small rain squall was moving across the ocean several hundred meters beyond the surf, sliding along with the first push of the morning's tradewinds. I watched it for a moment, trying to give my mind a moment to understand the "we" this old guy had just thrown at me.*

*"This is my dream," I continued. "I don't understand why you are in my dream." The words sounded a little harsh. He turned to look at me again.*

*"Not that you aren't welcome, of course," I added.*

*The old guy looked a little sad at that, picked up a small piece of coral off the sand, and took to twirling it in his hands. "Come on," he whispered. "I don't look that different do I?"*

*I shook my head in confusion and raised my eyebrows in question.*

"It's a little shocking to me too, actually," he said. "You're so damn young, and strong. I mean, look at you! Your arms could paddle Waimea - no problem." He turned back to look at the surf, still perfect, still glassy and still empty. "I had a hell of a time just getting into the one wave that I managed to catch, and it's only head high out there."

The old guy hung his head a moment. He let the piece of coral fall from his fingers.

"Should I know you?" I asked, still quite clueless to his many clues. My eyes caught the rain squall moving in a little closer, down the beach it was already pouring, but only in the next cove. The warmth on my back was still assuring me we would be safe from a soaking for now.

The old man folded his hands on his knees and avoided my eyes. "Mirrors are bad liars, except when they cross decades."

Something began seeping into my mind now. I looked at him to confirm what I was beginning to think. Oh my god!

"Actually, looking back on it all, I've got to give you a lot of credit," he said softly. He seemed to be trying to control his emotions, but I still detected a small tear pooling on his lower eyelids. "Despite all the pressure to do otherwise, you kept true to your dream. This dream."

A huge rainbow was beginning to pour out of the sky where the rain squall remained parked over the next cove. The brightness of the colors, the shimmering, was so vibrant I felt I could actually hear it.

"Thank you," the old man said.

"Am I," I asked, finally understanding. "Am I dreaming of you ... well, are you me ... as an old man?"

"Dreaming?" the old man said more than questioned. "I wouldn't quite call it a dream. I know I'm not dreaming." He looked over at the rainbow that was almost shouting at us. Suddenly, he stood, brushed the sand off his surf trunks, looking again toward the rainbow.

I stood up as well, brushing the sand off the backs of my legs.

"Yes," he now explained. "I am you, as a much older man, obviously. Today is my 100$^{th}$ birthday, and this is my present to myself." He took a few steps toward the water, and I followed, mesmerized.

"You look ... good," I muttered, trying real hard to say something and not freeze up in astonishment. I still couldn't quite believe it and was trying to pick out familiar parts of him that I might recognize better. His feet looked like mine, his hands not as much. His hair was still curly, if not some serious shades lighter.

Turning to me he almost put out his hand, and then withdrew it quickly. "You're so young," he grinned. "You're still learning to fly rainbows!" His laugh suddenly sounded very familiar, exactly like the one I heard when watching a DVD of myself telling jokes at a birthday party recently. "Oh, by the way," he continued. "Thanks for inventing that."

*Flying rainbows? What the hell was he saying?*

"What are you talking about?" I asked as he started to walk down the beach.

"Oh, that's going to be a while yet. Brilliant though. Good job!" He moved away from me, making some distance toward the rainbow that was now impacting the beach only a few dozen meters down the beach. I could feel little sprinkles of rain floating over like snow might in a breeze.

I watched him as he strode confidently down the sand. He looked damn good if he was actually 100 today. Damn good. I stood a little taller for a moment, somehow proud of myself.

Suddenly, he stopped, turned back to me and yelled. "Keep drinking that coconut water!"

He waved and walked briskly now, heading directly into the rainbow that had somehow brightened even further. I could hear the rain now and it was moving toward me, and about to engulf the old man.

I glanced over at the surf quickly, hearing another wave crack hard on the reef. The water was choppy now, and metallic gray as the squall moved closer and closer. The wind suddenly pushed into me, cold and wet. I looked back toward the old man, but the rain must be so thick it was hiding him. The rainbow was pulling back and in a few seconds was gone as the squall moved on top of me, and my dream. I stood my ground, getting soaking wet, afraid to turn and run.

"Honey ... honey!" Sandy was gently pushing against my shoulder. "Wake up."

I felt her pulling me back to the hammock, the warm sun and what I knew better as reality.

"You must have been having a good dream," Sandy said, her big brown eyes sparkling as she knelt down next to me. She was holding a tall smoothie of some kind.

"Really?" I asked, rubbing my eyes. "Why?"

She handed me the smoothie and waited for me to sit up a little higher in the hammock. "Because, darling, you were singing."

# DOUBLE ALOHA

It was late on a Thursday afternoon in Lahaina. As in most bars, things were slower than they would be the next day. Down the street, the other establishments were trying to entice customers in the door with various promotions.

One had a "Ladies Night", which had the strange effect of attracting far more men than women. It was, I was told, their worst night for fights. In theory, the idea was to entice women in with free drinks, followed by a herd of retail paying men. Those two effects effectively parlayed the crowd down to two types: wild women and highly competitive men. Quite similar to throwing a steak into a den of lions, the winners were the ones that didn't play fair. Sharing is not a natural instinct in the carnivore universe. Or in drinking establishments.. Lots of fights.

Another bar offered discounted drinks but had the bad habit of watering down the liquor bottles. It was, and this I was told as well having no direct knowledge, their most profitable night, on a drink by drink basis.

Yet another establishment at the far end of Front Street paraded scantily clad women in a "fashion show" from 4 PM until 5, then muscular men until 6 PM. After 6, most of their patrons then ran down to the "Ladies Night" bar.

Tiwaka's Tiki Bar & Grill didn't go for any of that bait and switch. We had "People's Night", every night. If you were a "people", you got in free. All week long. Watering down drinks was a sin of the highest order. In fact, we were famous for pouring strong drinks. As for scantily clad women and muscular men... well, we had a very colorful parrot. That would have to suffice. It usually did.

However, the reality of slow Thursdays was just as real here as elsewhere down Front Street. So, we invented "Double Aloha" night. The concept went like this: a free first drink went to any and all patrons, all night long, if they could describe how they had seen one good deed lead to another.

As bartender, I went first.

"OK," I said as I finished polishing some glassware. "Driving to work, I stopped to let some tourists jaywalk on Front street. One of them was super old, slow and dropped his hat right in the middle of the street. So, with all that extra time I took the opportunity to look around. Guess what?"

The four others in the bar at this early hour knew the game well.

"What? What did you see?"

"I looked up to the sky and saw Tiwaka flying in great big circles with some of his Waikiki buddies. It put me in the perfect mood for work."

I could tell they weren't too impressed with that, but it was all I had from this morning.

"My turn," the overly tanned tourist lady yelled, holding her hand up high.

"OK, OK," I pointed at her. "What you got, girl?"

She smiled as all eyes turned to her. Sitting up straighter on the bar stool she fidgeted with the ring on her right hand.

"I went into the ABC store for some Ocean vodka and this handsome local boy assisted me. He was so nice, I tipped him with the change. As I was leaving I saw him call over a small boy who was standing outside and whispered to him to go get some ice cream."

"Double Aloha!" everyone chanted.

Her overly tanned arm went up in the air again, as I nodded to her to continue.

"I'm going back tonight, when he's working to see if he can recommend some *massage oil*."

The raucous laughter set her eyes ablaze, giving her the group's approval to act on her idea. She was not unattractive, and she was certainly a friendly type. Also, her plan was certainly not outside the realm of what warm sunshine and tropical air seemed to encourage. It could work.

Three other hands went up. It was a slow evening which had the same advantage as a small classroom. Everyone had a chance.

I pointed toward the pineapple delivery guy who was using his evening break time to enjoy a smoothie I had just spun up for him.

"I was driving in from Kapalua and let this tour bus merge into my lane when no one else would. He honked his horn, waved at me and not much farther down the road, he let someone merge in front of him." He shrugged his shoulders. "Does that count?"

"Double Aloha!" we all cheered.

"Ah, darn," one of the remaining bar patrons sighed. "I had the same story. Beer truck."

The last person was about fifty years old and was new to the bar. He looked to be a tourist, but I wasn't sure. I nodded to him as I began preparing everyone's free first drinks.

"About twenty years ago, I was surfing, not far from here." He pointed north. "The waves were giant already that morning. Many of the guys in the water seemed unprepared. So many guys were getting cleaned up by the big sets."

He asked me for a glass of water. I could tell he was having a bit of trouble holding his composure.

"Several of us big wave guys were hanging way outside together, talking and shaking our heads at those dweebs that should have never been in the water in the first place." He looked around to the group. "Typical jock talk, you know," he added trying to soften up his tone.

"Suddenly, as can sometimes happen, a really, really big set of waves began piling up on the outer reef. All of us in my group began scrambling for the horizon, hoping as we paddled faster and faster that we could at least crest the top of the first monster."

He paused and took a long drink of the water. His hand was shaking a bit.

"We all made it over... well, actually I had to punch through the feathering top of it. As we all practically fell off the back of this first wave, we saw that the next one was even bigger. It was already throwing off a huge head of spray as the wind it was pushing rushed up and over.

"I looked quickly to my left and right. Several of the guys were already positioning themselves for the inevitable. I kept paddling.

Faster than I can remember. For some reason, I had to get over the top. As the mountain of water began carrying us all up, the guys all started bailing off their boards and diving as deep as they could. I quickly decided to keep trying to trying to get over the top. On my previous surf session, I had bailed off my board on a similar wave. I spent the next twenty minutes trying to save my ass from drowning. I didn't want to do that again."

I looked quickly at everyone as they watched him speak. They were fascinated, but the overly tanned tourist lady was mesmerized. She had her arms crossed over her chest, almost squeezing her ribs as he spoke. The pineapple delivery guy was nodding in agreement at every detail, no doubt having had a similar experience at one time or another. I had my own stories of terrifying surf adventures and could sympathize with his decision to hold onto his board.

"Amazingly enough, I made it through the top two feet of this breaking behemoth and blinded by a face full of blowing spray began descending rapidly down the back. The water's surface on the back of the wave looked like brushed cobalt steel. A continuous sheet of steel. No one was surfacing. My friends were all getting pummeled.

"I looked up for the third wave..." he paused again, drank a bit more water and looked at me.

I nodded to continue. We were all too invested in this story now to complain about its length. He smiled a bit and nodded ever so subtly back at me.

"The third wave was just as big as the second one, but with one perfect exception. I was in position to ride this one! Back in the day, even after all the adrenalin and fear and the mad scramble to get to this point, I wasn't exhausted. I was pumped up! Quickly turning my board back toward shore I began paddling again, as fast as I could. If I could match the thirty mile an hour speed of this rolling mountain I would have an easier time catching it.

"Catching the last wave in a big clean-up set is strange. No one is in your way, no one is paddling up to clear the wave you want. Inside further, toward the beach, it was nothing but apocalyptic rolling and surging boils of white water. Just beyond that were the green cliffs and sugar cane fields, held firmly in place by the dark tropical mountains in the distance, all topped with white trade wind clouds." He shook his head in amazement, even at his own words. "Beautiful. Even as I knew guys were getting thrashed inside, maybe even getting hurt. Yet," he paused, a glimmer in his eye. "Every one of them would be cheering me on if they could… if they could breathe. Every one of them…"

He jumped to his feet, climbed up on the stool and held a classic surfing stance. "Every one of them would take that drop!" He whooped it up loud and flexed his knees to the cheers of everyone, especially the overly tanned tourist lady.

"I was already sliding down the face of this monster. It roared all around me, intent on either killing me or testing my courage, or both." He suddenly stood up straight and looked at the overly tanned tourist lady. "I gotta tell you, though. I was scared to death!"

I watched them both, seeing the familiar signs often seen in bars. Infatuation and flirtation. God bless 'em both.

"I was trying my best to keep my balance as I navigated the steepening wall of this thing, even going around two abandoned surfboards. Behind me, it was already throwing out to form a barrel, but 'massive cave' might better describe it. I could hear it churning and compressing more and more air. This thing was bigger now than the first two waves. Easily!"

He jumped a few inches above the stool and landed with his feet in a different position, flexed his knees and held both hands high above his head.

"But, when the shadow crossed over me, I knew the wave was allowing me to ride inside of her." He glanced quickly to the overly tanned tourist lady with a big dose of mischievousness in his eyes. "All I had to do is respect her." He winked at her.

"And, not fall off!"

At that he jumped off the stool and sat back down on it.

"After that wild ride, I was far inside the bay. So was just about every other surfer who had been cleaned up by the three massive waves. Guys were struggling to get back on their boards and either paddle back out or straight in to the beach. Most were doing the later.

"That's when I heard a cry for help. It was the hoarseness in his voice that told me he was close to being done. I was also paddling in, but stopped and sat up on my board, trying to hear where the voice was coming from. The ocean was still boiling from my wave's collapse, but I finally saw a hand reach up, actually just the fingers on a hand, barely making it above all the foam.

"Quickly, I paddled over but the hand had disappeared. I put my head underwater but couldn't see anything except foam. After a moment, I saw the fingers again, ten feet away. They looked half curled up as they sank under the foam again. I dove off my board and swam down toward where they had disappeared."

He paused and shook his head.

"I thought the guy was already dead when I pulled him up onto my board. Another guy helped me get him to shore. That's where I gave him the mouth-to-mouth. It wasn't pretty. Took me quite a while to get him going again.

"Finally, he turned his head, threw up a gallon of seawater and took a big breath. And another. The guy had just got married the day before. Anthony Cabral. Said I saved his life.

"I guess I did." He stopped and looked down to his hands. He was trying to get his composure again.

"What happened to him?" The overly tanned tourist lady was on the edge of her seat. I was leaning on the bar.

"This was twenty years ago," his hands talking for him now. "I can still see it so clearly." Taking another sip of his water, he added. "He went on to have a great life and a family."

We all murmured approval, happy to hear a good ending to what could have been a sad story. I turned to make a few more drinks.

"Wait," he said softly. "There's more."

I glanced at everyone else. They were ready to afford him another moment, but we all felt the story now might turn a bit darker.

He looked at me, sheepishly.

"I went surfing in that same spot yesterday. It was giant, just like that day. I had to bail off my board for a big set, I just couldn't paddle fast enough to get over the top. It didn't go well. I got exhausted pretty quickly, getting tumbled on the inside and unable to get to the top of all that foam…"

He was on the verge of breaking down. The overly tanned tourist lady got off her stool and walked over to him, putting her hand on his shoulder as he tried to continue. In a moment, he managed to do so.

"Some guy rescued me, pulled me on to his board, gave me mouth-to-mouth on the rocks. He had to bang on my chest. Said later he wasn't sure I was going to come back.

"Obviously, I did." He wiped a small tear from the corner of his eye. "I finally got enough breath back to thank him, and ask his name."

The overly tanned tourist lady squeezed his arm and patted him on the back.

"Who was he? A lifeguard?" she asked softly.

He nodded, shook his head, nodded again and unsuccessfully tried to suppress a sob. We all waited patiently as he worked through it.

"Anthony Cabral."

The overly tanned tourist lady began crying and hugging him. Everyone started clapping and cheering. But, he tried to stop us by raising his hand. We quieted.

"Junior."

That put us all over the top. People out on Front Street, shopping for t-shirts and eating ice cream all paused as they heard screams and clapping inside our nearly empty bar. A small girl listened closely to the racket, her ice cream melting all over her fingers. When her brother asked her what we were saying, she answered with a look of amazement on her face.

"Double Aloha."

# LONELY HEARTS CLUB

My brother, the vacationing astronaut, came into the bar every night since our opening week. But, he didn't stay long. He sat at a stool on the end, absentmindedly feeding Tiwaka chocolate covered cashews, scanning the crowd for someone.

He wouldn't say who, in fact, he didn't admit to even looking for someone. I didn't press him on the matter. If anything he needed to relax. As long as he was at sea level, along with the rest of us, I had no complaint. He would adjust, eventually.

Alana was the only one who knew who he was looking for. She tried to explain it all to me, but with Tiwaka's continuous interruptions, I was having a difficult time following her story. Something about a woman of extraordinary beauty, someone to be avoided, but someone quite impossible to ignore. That's if you could even see her in the first place.

Finally, I threw a cashew across the room for Tiwaka to follow, turned to Alana and stared at her with some irritation.

"Are you telling me only you and Hudson can see this woman?"

"I know, it sounds crazy. I've got no explanation. I've only got what I know. Hudson saw her walk into the bar his first night here. I saw her too." She looked down at her feet, then over to the window before finally finding my eyes boring into her. "No one else paid any attention to her. No one else could see her."

Alana put her empty tray down on the bar and leaned in to whisper.

"She's exotic. Something beyond sexual, but full of that energy too, of course. Lots of it. If you watch her eyes, and she looks at you…" Alana paused and swallowed. She appeared to be sweating ever so slightly above her eyebrows. "She's intoxicating."

"Intoxicating?" I repeated. "Surely, I would have noticed her, Alana. Why didn't I see her?"

Alana was reaching over the bar, pulling cold Primos off of my counter and piling them onto her tray. She didn't look at me.

"I don't know. Lucky, I guess." She picked up her tray and made a move to the nearest table.

"Wait."

She turned back to me, frustration and a big hint of sadness on her face.

"Why would it be lucky for me not to see her?" I immediately felt like I shouldn't have asked that question. The frown on her face confirmed it was a mistake.

Alana walked back to the bar and sat her tray down on the bar. I could see her measuring her response against our established level of employer-employee familiarity.

I tried to look approachable.

She put her hands under the tray and as she lifted it up again, she whispered just loud enough for me to hear her above the noise.

"She's a heart breaker. That's why."

~~~

The sidewalks of Lahaina were full of so many people, yet completely empty. Empty realizations. The feet that marched there knew nothing. Nothing about why their feet were pressed against the cracked concrete. Sure, someone might claim gravity, but they would be using the word in a context of ignorance. Ignorance based in never knowing the absence of gravity. Never knowing the real reason it existed in the first place.

I paused for a moment outside my brother's Tiki bar, in that special area under the Monkeypod tree. Where the sand met the soil, where the hobos sometimes slept.

My eyes softly closed, ignoring the distractions, the human drama all around me. I slowly pulled a rush of fragrant air into my lungs, feeling it settle deep inside of me.

The weight felt so comforting. The weight of the Earth, pulling me toward its breast, wanting only love.

It hugged me like a small child, one trapped in an adult's body, without any judgment. The warm dirt between my toes, the distant voices drifting on a gentle breeze, all caressed my skin with the soft textures of land and atmosphere.

The sun had already fallen below the horizon, allowing the vastness of star-filled space to flow in all around me. I welcomed it, its kiss against my skin. A few others seemed to notice as well, mostly kids.

The last of the reluctant street lights along Front Street flickered on. Moving away into a shadow, I looked up into the sky. In space, the beauty was always distant. The stars glared their stark beacons into the vacuous ink, screaming their songs against the black silence.

But, down here, below the fading, light-blue glow of oxygen and nitrogen and hydrogen, the thickness of air diffused our own star's scream until it could only be described as the secret whispered song of a lover.

I longed for that whisper. That song.

It was nice to be home.

Crossing the street I walked quietly into Tiwaka's Tiki Bar & Grill, looking again for Tatiana.

~~~

Friday night and things were hopping.

But, not for Hudson.

Alana confirmed that the mystery woman was not around. She tried to cheer him up, even distract him. I could see she felt some level of competition from the exotica this mystery woman had cast on my brother.

I wasn't sure if Alana actually had a crush on Hudson or that her attraction to him was due to their mutual fascination with some almost magical creature that only they could see.

Of course, just thinking that had me shaking my head. Both of them were probably not reliable witnesses to reality. My brother was on psychological leave after being stranded in orbit for a year and a half. And, Alana had been stranded on Maui for her entire twenty-something years.

Sanity was overrated, but having worked in this business for so long I understood that it was best to never let anyone else really know how tight your grasp was or wasn't on it. Most folks failed at that.

Hudson finally left the bar, but I secretly followed him for a block or so until it was obvious he was OK. He slowly moved through the throngs of people until he found a comfortable spot against the sea wall.

I watched him for a full five minutes until I was convinced he was safe, non-suicidal and most importantly, above the high tide line.

Mom had always said he was prone to daydreaming. As I turned away I knew that him staring up into the sky was harmless.

I wondered if he missed it.

# SUB-ORBITAL EPIPHANIES

Above Earth.

We've all done it. A thousand times. Stood at some altitude above the ground and looked around. On a ladder, in a treehouse, a tall building or most likely from an airplane. There is a shared commonality in the view we find there. They all lend themselves to a keen appreciation of gravity even as we attempt to defy it.

Gravity.

It doesn't give up. Ever. Regardless of where you place the soles of your feet, in the grass or in seat 19A. Look around, as far as you can see. You always know that the dominant direction is down. Gravity.

Trying to get away from it altogether proves no casual feat. At launch, it's absolutely overwhelming. Not unexpected. Training gives us an edge, of course. Yet, the fear is always sequestered off in a corner of our minds. In a glass box. Where we can still see the contents. I liked the way that worked. I always knew where it was, didn't have to worry about it getting loose. That left me enough bandwidth to focus on the important stuff. Like: 'I hope the damn engines don't burp, that the caulking on the windscreen was up to spec, and that the pressure on my crotch would let up enough for me to readjust.'

Down always wants you back. Jump all you want, Down wins and keeps you there. Until you jump again. Jump with enough energy, say escape velocity and Down has to pause. It doesn't quit mind you, just pauses while you propel yourself up at just over 7 miles per second. That's a difficult speed to imagine, at first.

In a commercial jet, you travel 10 miles in sixty seconds. Escape velocity would get you 420 miles in that same minute. Straight up. Yes, it's noisy. And bumpy. And terrifying.

There, I said it. We all feel it, admittedly or not. Some astronauts like it. I never did. My mind was always counting the seconds until the last burn was finished and I could move into freefall.

Endless freefall.

If you're a skydiver you drool at the thought. It can be intoxicating. Eventually. After your heave for the first two or three days, you get your space legs. Similar to getting one's sea legs on a boat. Until that happens you could swear it was your stomach misbehaving. No, it's just a brain thing. It takes that long for our brains to adjust to significantly new stimuli. Get new glasses lately? Notice how it takes a few days to get comfortable with them, especially if bifocals are blended into the glass. Similarly, babies see their parents upside down for the first three days. The software your brain came installed with figures it out by then, righting a world that our corneas forever invert through optics.

In zero gravity, or what we call zero because it's so close, our brains work the same magic. First timers will eventually experience 'the adjustment', a shedding of the skin. Euphemistically, of course, but it feels the same. The irritating stress of that falling feeling vaporizes like a sudden chill in the warm sun. For me, the first time I adjusted was magical. I had just unhooked myself from the wall after a rest period and was making my way to relieve myself. Day 3. Very first space flight. My mind was still spending a lot of energy dealing with vertigo. It wasn't the first time I had experienced it. Certainly not. Training was full of moments like this. However, now it wouldn't stop. Training in zero-G was always brief. Twenty seconds here, another twenty several minutes later. This was unending.

But, as I passed the Russian module I felt something click. I felt better, suddenly a lot better. My movements, bouncing my way down the passage, became more fluid, easier. And, when I paused at a porthole and saw the blue Pacific below, sliding so smoothly by, I finally got it. I was flying. Not falling.

And that was far cooler.

Until it wasn't.

Leaving the space station and dropping into a sub-orbital trajectory always brought back the falling sensation, for me anyhow. It was exactly like wiping out on the black diamond ski slopes. You were already going too fast when you lose the smooth surface of your skis and begin descending on your butt, and back.

It's slightly rough and bouncy. Uncomfortable. Like the turbulence over the Rockies that disturbs your airline nap. Steady, and building. You can't see what's ahead, but you know. It's gonna get worse. A lot worse. Imagine how bad it is when the airline captain's announcement tells the flight attendants to stop serving lunch and to sit down. Well, descent from orbit is so bad they don't even let the flight attendants get on board in the first place.

You feel the violence increase steadily. On the black diamond, you're now hoping you can just stay out of the trees.

You can't see the bottom yet, but as you plow through the powder, thin and wispy like the upper atmosphere, you feel yourself working lower, toward the hard snow pack.

The shaking is unnerving. You try to measure its frequency, referencing yet again the training you've had. The simulator. You remember the technicians reluctantly admitting that it would be slightly different in the field. A bit worse. Still, the shaking was beyond anything your new Ford-tough truck could endure. How any man-made machine could endure the abuse was a marvel of engineering. Of course, when it's your ass inside that marvelously engineered machine it's nothing short of a miracle.

This last re-entry had been particularly stressful. We were already in overspeed, overshooting our first waypoint. Who knows why. That discussion would be held after I landed this thing.

We still had several options. But we were now down one. We had to bleed off some speed, but until the air thickened, which would slow us enough to use our wings and elevator we could only hang on. Another minute and we had overshot our second waypoint too early. Now things were getting dicey. Getting behind a machine moving this fast could seriously compromise your next meal.

The atmosphere above Hawaii finally started taking a bite of our speed, slowing us enough to where I could feel the controls vibrating and then swimming through the air. I nodded to my brother's Tiki Bars below.

My Boeing passenger, a prize-winning employee, had a worried look on his face. I probably did as well. California was no longer an option. Texas was rapidly approaching. That left Florida.

In a small RTE vehicle such as ours, we had a dozen options beyond what the old space shuttles used to have. All of them really poor: abandoned military runways and even stretches of Interstates 80, 40 and 10. Like I said, really poor choices.

These machines were not much bigger than a Piper Cherokee. Space X had just delivered two to the space station. Someone had figured it was cheaper this way since they could be folded back into a cube for reuse on another later descent. RTEs were still not heavily trusted in the astronaut community. Return To Earth was about all it would guarantee. In one piece or in ashes, it was going to return to Earth alright.

For some reason, I flashed back on my early sailplane adventures and one in particular. I had borrowed the local, retired United pilot's brand new Grob aerobatic machine, promising he could trust me if NASA had just hired me. He sized me up, took my picture next to his glider and smiled.

All went well until it was time to land. The tradewinds suddenly accelerated at that remote Hawaiian airfield and my first bad decision soon became evident. I, being a bit lazy, had decided to land mid-field instead of at the beginning of the runway. This way I wouldn't have to pull the glider farther than necessary back to the hanger. So, as I turned base and lined up with mid-field I noticed my airspeed rapidly increase. Fortunately, I had extra altitude. I had wanted to practice a dive bomb approach anyhow. Just a few seconds later I was beyond any hope of making mid field and was looking at a rapidly approaching end-of-the-runway scenario. No engine available for a go around.

Gliders. That's all they do, glide. Every landing was an emergency landing, powered by the pull of gravity.

This descent from orbit was exactly the same. I wasn't going to make a landing where I wanted to unless I could somehow slow down. Way, way down.

The controls were now finally responsive so I clicked off the auto-pilot. The Boeing guy next to me noticed and tightened his belts.

"Are we...?" his voice barely made it above the din.

"Altitude and airspeed!" I commanded. "Yell them out continuously!"

He didn't say anything until I turned quickly to catch his eye.

"Now! Keep saying them until we land!"

I felt us veer to the right slightly. Damn! I had memorized all the headings I needed. Right now, I needed 082 degrees. I moved the stick slightly to the left. I couldn't perform speed-bleeding turns quickly enough without over-stressing the wings

"52,000. 800 knots," the Boeing employee yelled out.

According to the flight computer, I needed to be at 675 knots... about a thousand miles ago.

Back at Dillingham airfield, in that spiffy and borrowed Grob, I knew what I had to do to keep it out of the mud just beyond the runway. I pulled back on the stick. Enough to approach a stall, killing my forward speed. It had worked then. It would work again. Hopefully.

My hand gently pulled the control stick back toward my crotch.

"41,500. 720 knots!"

I pulled back a little harder, feeling the reluctant elevator do as it was asked.

"36,000. 700 knots!"

The flight computer had me overshooting all but the last two approved landing strips. Miami International and Kennedy Space Center just up the coast. Miami was problematic. Kennedy was going to have to be it. But, the computer was saying I should have been at 23,500 and 400 knots at this point.

"31,500. 690 knots!"

Houston was demanding to know if everything was OK. "Roger" was all they got.

I pulled back on the stick, much harder now, setting off stall warnings and turning the Boeing guy an interesting shade of green.

"Altitude!" I shouted at his hesitation.

"22,000. 550 knots! What the hell..."

This was going to get me fired if not dead. Some NASA manager was going to say I should have aborted at the first missed waypoint and attempted the Azores emergency site. That was a bad idea. Lots of lonely ocean between Kennedy and the Portuguese islands. At least they'd find our bodies if we crashed over land. Besides I wanted shrimp and beer tonight, not massa sovada and port.

I felt the bottom fall out of our RTE. We were beginning to stall.

The Boeing guy was screaming now.

"15,000. 250 knots!"

Enough. I pushed the stick forward again. Our airspeed quickly picked up again.

"11,500. 375 knots!"

The warning bells had stopped and the flight computer showed our new trajectory very close to what was required.

"8,000. 395 knots." His voice was calming down a bit.

Nice. The wings hadn't ripped off and I could see the runway. Those iconic Florida pine trees were standing proud as we swept past them.

The Boeing guy, who had only just flown up on the same supply ship that brought my long awaited relief crew, seemed anxious to get his lips pressed to the ground immediately after our stairs deployed against the hot, summer-cooked runway. I watched him barf a moment later.

Best day of his life.

I just sat in my seat, waiting for the extraction crew I most certainly needed. Earth welcomed me back with a full one-G super-hug and I could barely move.

I sat patiently.

My breathing was slowly calming along with my heartbeat. The ground crew was a little slow hooking up some air conditioning which proved I could still sweat. They would be a couple of more minutes. My helmet slid off my damp hair easily. After shutting down the final electrical subsystem, I finally relaxed. Enough to suck in a long breath of fresh, ocean kissed air. I had earned it, through confidence and creativity.

It would be shrimp and beer tonight.

Nice.

I pulled out my iPod, jacked into the AUX port and blasted my current favorite: "Beat the Devil's Tattoo". Looking out the front windows I could see I still had half the runway left.

Real nice.

# BANYAN TREE FLIGHT SCHOOL

Tiwaka was as proud as a peacock. His flight school was a great success. He and his new Waikiki friends quickly made the giant banyan tree in Lahaina their training facility. It took three months, but the flightless sidewalk-performance macaws finally grew their wings out enough to fly.

Watching them cavort around the branches, competing with the resident Mynah bird village for attention, was like watching teenagers at a school dance. Most of them held back, but a few brave ones danced in the open, where everyone could see and eventually find encouragement to do the same.

Naturally, Tiwaka danced first, by himself. He wasn't a particularly good dancer, but he made up for that with an unbridled enthusiasm that soon convinced you he might actually be the best dancer that had ever moved their feet.

Moments later, and this happened every night at sunset, the entire tree was rocking. Hundreds of birds were singing, talking and jumping about. The air pulsed with the fluttering of their wings and I'm guessing the expansion of proud parrot chests.

Of course, Tiwaka and his Waikiki crew of rescued sidewalk parrots had every right to be proud. I had just sold their services to three Lahaina fishing boat captains, for a percentage of the catch.

Tiwaka and the Waikikians, as we called them now, would fly out from the giant Banyan tree when they heard the various captains' boat whistles. Launching into the early dawn light, long before the drunken

Mynah birds would even think of stirring, they climbed high into the cool island air. Tiwaka always in the lead of a rather loose formation of other parrots, they all searched from a hundred feet up. Searched for schools of fish.

The Lahaina fishing boat captains, sometimes one, sometimes all three of them together, would watch the flock of colorful birds with binoculars. Often this involved motoring several miles out from the harbor, toward the island of Lana'i.

During the free trial I had offered, their success rate was double what they had experienced before the birds had been hired. All they had to do was watch for Tiwaka and the Waikikians to begin circling. Directly below would be the schools of fish the captains needed to feed the hungry tourists at Lahaina's various restaurants.

Every seaside restaurant in Lahaina now had a wealth of fresh fish selections. Anthony Bourdain's cooking and travel show came to town, raved about the menu in each and every establishment but never knew the real reason behind the extraordinarily good selection of seafood.

The Mynah birds, famous blabber mouths, were paid off to keep the secret. They had never eaten so well.

# PARADISE FOUND

"We did an extraordinary amount of good, but on a very small scale," Ma and Pa had said.  They were talking about their original Tiwaka's Tiki Bar & Grill out in the jungles of north Maui.  "You and your brother, this magical place, all of it has made us so happy.  So proud."

We were sitting up in the treehouse with a view of the surf flowing around the corner at Unknowns and the magnificent Haleakala mountain peak out the opposite windows.

"In all the universe, with all that is possible in such a vastness, we know we did our part.  Thanks to you boys," Pa waxed poetic at times.  I took the compliment and the hug with pleasure.

I was there on my weekly visit to gather coconuts for the Lahaina bar and to say hi.  Of course, Ma's breakfast bananas, homegrown strawberries, and free range chicken egg omelets were just a bonus.  OK, I'll admit it, but only to you folks:  it was my primary reason for visiting.  But, in my twisted logic, of which I am quite comfortable with, all my reasons were primary.  So, there!

My parents were happy as could be, but I could tell they were slowing down a bit as they got older.  Their scene there was comfortable, unstressful and they were often surrounded by the few fortunate friends they had visiting.

The sun had always risen with the chirping of birds and the still coolness of morning air from the sea, hovering just over and through the coconut trees.  Their days were full of warm diversions and naps and soft music, either from the radio or both of them singing while cooking in the kitchen. Late afternoons awarded them with visiting friends, more food, and ukuleles. Evenings were lit with a small bonfire, Tiki bar lamps, and storytelling, finished off with a resounding sing-a-long of some old favorite they all knew. The nights let them sleep nestled in the fragrances of night blooming flowers carried by cool tradewind breezes.

It was, at first glance, idyllic.

To me, it was beyond that. It was paradise.

Paradise.

The most overused, misunderstood and subjective concept this side of the moon. I had heard it whispered here in the tropics since I could remember. It was marketed heavily to those poor souls that considered themselves far away from it.

Often, after some thousands of dollars and a long plane ride they arrived here expecting "paradise" to run up to them with open lips, a big hug and promises of things exotic and forbidden. They expected "paradise" to be a magical version of some mythical Disney ride flavored with rum, sun, and promiscuity.

Hopes and promises being what may, that's not quite my definition. Paradise had nothing to do with the tropics or the beach or sex. Not that those three things couldn't participate, they just weren't necessarily required.

After loading the coconuts in the truck and kissing Ma on the cheek, I looked in on Pa taking a nap. All was well with them, but I had one more thing to do before I left.

I walked the narrow, muddy jungle path out to where Tiwaka and I had buried Ococ so many years ago. Pua'kinikini was blossoming along the way, feeding the honey bees and adding a sweetness to the cool tradewind brushed air. The sky was far more benign than the thunderous day we had laid him to rest. Today, with the distant mountain bamboo groves undulating to some song only they could hear, with the high ridges behind them entertaining small bursts of moisture laden air, with the quiet peacefulness all around, I exhaled.

Exhaled and sat down next to Ococ's grave.

The ground was moist, but I didn't care if my cargo shorts got damp. It felt good. Felt good to spend a moment remembering the old dog. It was also something else. It was peaceful. It was a happy place, not sad. Happy memories were all that remained of those times.

Peace. Happiness.

I think that's what I would call paradise.

~~~

Saturday night was looking super busy.

Alana was training two new helpers, the cooks in the kitchen had a new dishwasher and Sandy was working the bar with me. Baby Kiawe was with Ma and Pa for the weekend. Although I hated being away from him, I knew he would get more quality time with them than he would tied to a lease attached to a coconut tree behind the bar.

Wait, did I say that out loud?

No, of course, that was just a joke. Lahaina had a law specifically forbidding that. Coconut trees had been used in babysitting for years, but the times had changed. For the better. Of course.

Hudson wandered in around 8 P.M.

I waved him over just as Tiwaka launched from the vodka shelves behind me and headed straight for him. The crowd cheered thinking it was one of the bird's predictable flights announcing a fresh arrival of coconuts behind the bar. I had fresh cocos already, so I couldn't fault him for the false alarm.

Hudson saw the five foot wingspan approach from just over the heads of everyone and held his gloved hand up high. This wasn't his first rodeo. It was his second. The first one involved blood. After that, I told him what to expect from the crazy bird and gave him a stove mitt from the kitchen.

"Tiwaka cleared to land," Hudson joked as the talons gripped the mitt and big wings folded back along his sides.

"Hudson!" Tiwaka squawked. "10, 9, 8…"

The crazy bird had somehow figured out Hudson rode on rockets and having later watched a few YouTube videos learned that there was always a countdown involved. The bar crowd joined in.

"7, 6, 5…" Alana stopped and watched, as did her trainees. The guys from the kitchen ran out, wiping their hands on their white aprons before clapping with each number.

Sandy jumped up on the bar, much to the local wood cutter's in the place enjoyment. I did a double take as well. She looked great!

"4, 3, 2..." Tiwaka opened his wings again, as Hudson now held him high above his head.

The place was going nuts! I couldn't believe this many people could make this much noise.

"1! Blastoff!" Or something that sounded like that came from Tiwaka. Everyone else pronounced it perfectly.

Tiwaka launched himself up and away from Hudson, flew over everyone's head twice, snapping up whatever pretzels people threw up toward him, then came back to the bar for his victory march down the length of the bar.

Everyone there immediately covered their drinks with their napkins. Sandy climbed back down to give the bird some room and to ring the large brass ship's bell we had.

"A dollar off everyone's drinks for the next hour!" she announced to more cheers.

The bird was prancing down toward the wood cutters, wiggling his tail and bobbing his head. The cute girls sitting with them started screaming in excitement... just what Tiwaka loved. The higher pitch the better. I saw a bit of trouble, though. The girls were all wearing bikini tops with a draw string in the front.

"You've got quite a bird there, bro," Hudson laughed, making his way up to the waitress station. "I think a reality TV show might be in your future!"

"Yeah," I said. However, my distraction was in full throttle. I knew what Tiwaka was up to. So did the wood cutters who had been in last week and seen the trick before. No doubt they had suggested their dates dress exactly as they had.

"What's wrong?" Hudson asked, following my gaze.

"Nothing," I said. "As long as the health inspector is not in here." I looked around. I didn't see anyone that was trying to fake not being a health inspector. You could usually spot them a mile away. Always wearing impeccably clean clothing with a pocket protector.

"Is it Tiwaka?" Hudson asked. He turned to watch the bird as he let the bikini girls pat him on his feathered head. "What's he going to do?"

I looked at Hudson and with all the seriousness I could muster, most of it authentic, and said, "I didn't train him to do what he's about to do. OK?"

Hudson smiled broadly. "OK." He walked behind the bar with me and stood behind my shoulder. I could hear him say "This ought to be good!"

It would be.

The girls were practically giggling, stroking the bird's feathers from his head down his back to his gyrating tail. It was a provocative show by Tiwaka and meant to distract.

The wood cutters and the regulars in the bar who knew what was coming got their camera phones ready. Sandy turned her head, trying to control her laughter. She didn't quite approve but knew Tiwaka's antics were harmless.

We would see.

The hibiscus bedecked girl, his first target, had moved right up against the bar, her belly button just below as she stood on the foot railing below

"Take my picture!" she laughed. "Take my picture!"

Everyone who was in on the trick were waiting for Tiwaka's cue.

Her two girlfriends moved in close, to photobomb her. Perfect, I could just hear Tiwaka thinking. He cocked his head back, squawked painfully loud, which was the cue, and took a step toward the first girl. In an instant, he had tugged her drawstring loose, letting the cups of her bikini top fall to the sides. In half a second more he had sidestepped to the first friend and did the same. By the time the third girl saw it coming she couldn't move fast enough.

In two seconds, Tiwaka had rendered topless three girls at the bar. The flashes from the camera phones were almost blinding. Sandy and I both swooped in before the girls could get angry. I grabbed the bird and Sandy put three free drinks in front of the girls as they quickly tied their tops back together.

Everyone at the bar was clapping and congratulating the girls.

"You're initiated now! Gold member!" The wood cutters were saying. People were patting them on the shoulders, telling them what good sports they were.

As soon as I had placed Tiwaka back among the vodka bottles I ran over and profusely apologized.

"He's been under a lot of stress," I began. "It's actually documented behavior for his species under these circumstances."

The wood cutters were trying to stand back so their dates wouldn't see them laughing. They had heard me go through this routine before.

"What circumstances are that?" One of the girls was none too happy about it all. The other two were still laughing.

"I'm so, so sorry," I said with my best apologetic face. "Whenever Tiwaka is in close proximity to beautiful women, especially as gorgeous as you ladies are, he gets unpredictable. I promise he won't do it again."

She didn't seem too impressed.

"Free drinks for you ladies, and dinner, on me. Rest of the night. OK?"

That worked.

But, I saw her tie another extra knot in her top.

# KAHIKI NUI

The night was progressing by the playbook.

People were eating, drinking and being quite merry. Tiwaka was getting tired and found that sitting in the corner was a fine way to relax. Sandy and I were mixing, pouring, slicing, dicing and occasionally stealing a kiss or three. It was almost 11.

Alana was standing at the waitress station when I looked up from the ice well.

"What you need, Alana?" I asked, filling cocktail glasses with fresh ice.

"She's here," she said very softly. I had to ask her to repeat it.

"What?" I stood up straight and looked her in the eye. She was almost afraid, or maybe it was nervousness.

"Hudson's friend," she said. Her hands were fidgeting with a toothpick.

"The intoxicant?" I joked. "Point her out to me."

Alana quickly turned toward the corner of the bar next to the street and close to the door. She pointed.

"There's Hudson. She's right next to him."

I tried to look through the crowd and the blinking Tiki lights. Nothing. No Hudson, no exotic invisible beauty.

"Where, Alana? I don't even see Hudson."

She grabbed my arm.

"Follow me, I'll show you."

I signaled Sandy that I was leaving the bar and followed Alana. The crowd was in full dance mode, moving between the tables, onto the dance floor and blocking our path to Hudson.

I still couldn't see him.

Leaning over I yelled above the noise into Alana's ear.

"Are you sure?"

She just pulled my hand harder. We got about halfway through the dancers and I think I spotted Hudson, standing up and walking toward the door.

"I see him!" He looked like he was smiling.

"She's holding his hand, do you see her?" Alana pulled me faster toward the door.

I couldn't see anyone holding my brother's hand. Then I lost sight of Hudson again in the crowd.

"Hurry, I think he's leaving." I could hear the excitement in my own voice.

Alana stopped and looked me in the eye, clutching my hand so firmly I wanted to pull it back.

"*They're* leaving!"

I shook my head in some confusion. I didn't see any *they* and I didn't even see Hudson.

We moved to the edge of the dance floor and then made for the exit. I saw Hudson then, just moving through it, as well as a dozen others. We were out the door ourselves a moment later. Alana let go of my hand and stood there, hands on her hips.

"Well, do you see them now?"

I looked at the crowds, the sidewalks and the bicycles navigating between them all. Finally, I saw Hudson. By himself.

"I see Hudson..."

Alana was exasperated. "They're holding hands for God's sake!"

I looked again, and for a moment, just a moment, I thought I saw someone there. Long flowing black hair, his height, her hand in his. But, it passed quickly, as if I had blinked and she was gone. Which is exactly what happened.

Hudson moved down the stairs off the sidewalk and down toward the tiny beach just in front of the sea wall. Then he was gone as well.

Alana turned, stood on her toes and held me by the shoulders.

"Well? Did you see her?"

I looked into her eyes, wanting to answer that I did, but I wasn't sure. Maybe I wanted to see her and that's what I had seen. A hope, a manufactured vision that both Alana and I wanted me to see.

Her eyes were tearing now. I could only watch a second longer as one spilled out onto her cheek. My eyes moved away from hers.

"I think I did."

Alana let go of me and walked around behind me, back into the bar. I heard a sob as she passed me.

Turning quickly, I yelled out to her.

"I saw something…"

But she was gone too. Vanished into the bar.

"I did," I said to myself. "I saw something."

I just didn't know what it was. Standing there on the crowded sidewalk, people having to navigate around me, something told me to follow him, Hudson.

The bar would wait, but Sandy would probably complain. I'd have to make it up to her. Crossing the street, dodging a bicycle rider wearing some kind of hula skirt, I made my way to the sidewalk above the sea wall.

There, down on the beach, walking away, was Hudson. I didn't see anyone with him. Yet, his hand did appear to be out to the side, as if he might actually be holding someone's hand. That was surely a strange thing.

The lighting wasn't all that good, but I thought I could see a parallel set of footprints, next to his, in the sand. Of course, I reasoned, he might just be walking next to a previous set of prints created by someone a few moments ago.

Just as I was about to turn away and leave him to his loneliness, a tiny ankle high wave surged up the sand. It splashed on something next to him, before it reached him. Something that was between him and the water. Surely, my eyes and imagination were playing tricks on me in the bad lighting. Surely.

I moved toward the stairs, intent on running up to Hudson. My first step down was halted immediately. The ship's bell in the bar was being rung repeatedly. I turned and looked back toward Tiwaka's Tiki Bar & Grill.

Reality was calling. I had to answer.

~~~

I wanted to ask Tatiana where she had been for the last couple of weeks. I knew my brother and every regular in the bar probably thought I was being an idiot hoping some girl I met once would show back up. I know they had all cut me a lot of slack because of my being stuck in orbit. I had cut myself quite a bit of slack for that too. But, regardless of any and all accommodations, it had been too long to wait for a girl in a bar.

Tatiana turned to me, catching my thought in her soft smile. I stopped and stood transfixed.

"Were you waiting long, for me?"

"No," I said politely. Her eyes told me she knew the truth already. "Well, yes. I thought you might not come back at all."

She took my other hand and turned to me. The lights of the bars behind us cast a glow of softly brushed light against her skin. For some reason her eyes actually appeared to have a slight sparkle to them.

"I'm so sorry. I have a problem with time." She leaned in, kissed me quickly and pulled away. I followed her with my lips until I found she had moved back. "Relativity and all," she laughed softly.

As we continued to stand in the wet sand I could feel us sinking ever so slightly with each passing wave that lapped at our feet. I could also feel myself sinking, completely out of control. From waiting weeks for her to reappear to leaving the bar at her suggestion and then trying to follow her kiss to no avail.

I stepped back from her, up onto the dry sand. My watch alarm vibrated. Saved by the bell as it were.

"Come, I want to show you something," I asked her. "Up there in the sky."

Standing next to me she followed my hand as I found, and then followed a rapidly moving light, no brighter than a star, crossing from southeast to northwest, directly above us.

"I used to live there." The pride in my voice was not exaggerated.

She wrapped her arms around my left arm and squeezed slightly. Her head leaned against my shoulder. When I glanced at her, those eyes of hers were following the light as it raced toward the horizon.

"On a satellite?"

I nodded. It was technically just that.

"The International Space Station."

She continued following the ISS until it disappeared. I wasn't sure if she quite understood.

"Is that a lot like living underwater?"

Before I could answer, she added another question.

"Isn't it very small inside, like something underwater might be?"

"Yes, it is." I looked at the depth of the blackness above, fascinated still with the punctuation of lights afforded by all those thermonuclear reactions. "Except the view is better, I suspect."

Tatiana released my arm and took my hand.

"I have a view I'd like to show you. Can you swim?"

The waters off of Lahaina were inky black. My hesitation showed.

"It's not far, just out to my outrigger. You know, a canoe."

She looked at me expecting some reluctance. It was there alright, but I fought it back. It was past midnight, the ocean full of sharks and I didn't see any outrigger canoe.

"Where is it?" I asked suspiciously. "Are you trying to get me to go skinny dipping?" My nervous laugh didn't quite carry the joke.

She smiled at my attempt anyhow. I followed her into the shadow of an overhanging deck where the next set of shops along the waterfront began.

"Well, it is easier to swim that way." She reached up behind her neck and unhooked the pareo she was wearing, letting it fall into the sand. "We can leave our clothes here, I have more in the outrigger."

Even in the street light shadows, her nakedness was overwhelming. I followed her quickly, dropping my shirt and shorts on top of her pareo. It felt best to gather them all together and stash them up in a spot I found just under the deck.

She was already thigh high in the calm waters when she paused to look back for me. Second date and already naked in the ocean. I guess I could live with that.

Still watching me she pointed behind her.

"Can you see it? The outrigger canoe?"

I peeled my eyes away and searched the dark waters behind her. The slight movement of it on the water caught my attention first. A moment later, my mind painted a preconceived image of a Hawaiian style canoe, colorfully painted, two paddles propped against the inside railings.

"I'll follow you," I replied. Even into dark tropical waters, naked and vulnerable, I thought to myself. Damn. I fought the urge to go over a checklist before I accepted the risk. Yet, I couldn't help myself.

- Can I actually swim that far? CHECK
- Are there any obvious hazards between us and the canoe that a reasonable man would avoid? NEGATIVE
- Can I survive without a protective suit? ROGER
- Do I need anyone at NASA's approval? ....

Tatiana dove in, only her long black hair remaining a second longer above the surface. I moved a few feet deeper, prepared to do the same, but not until I had my answer to the last item on my checklist: HELL NO.

~~~

Alana avoided me until closing. Sandy saw that something was up between us and at her first opportunity asked about it.

"What's wrong with Alana? She looks upset."

Sandy had one hand on her hip, which was the secret body language precursor to an inquisition. Immediately, I knew my answer would have to include more information than the question framed. She'd also want to know why Alana pulled me outside during a busy rush at the bar, and why Alana came back first, while she had to ring the bell to get me to return.

Any pause to my answer would also invite more detailed questioning.

"She's convinced Hudson has a girlfriend. But, I never saw her."

Sandy shifted her hips to the other side, placed her other hand on that hip and raised an eyebrow. Obviously, my answer was flawed.

"And you both had to leave the bar during that rush, to what, say hi?"

I shook my head. There would be no good answer at this point. Especially the truth. But, the truth is always easier to remember later. So I went with that, for the most part.

"Alana says that Hudson is infatuated with some gorgeous local beauty. I thought that would be just what the doctor ordered for him. However, I never managed to see her. Alana thinks I'm blind, and insisted on showing her to me."

Both hands went to her hips now. I was toast.

"And? Did you see this, what did you call her, 'gorgeous local beauty'?"

Quickly, I saw my exit and played my ace card with perfect timing.

"Well, as I explained to Alana, there is no such thing as another gorgeous local beauty anywhere in whatever timezone you, my darling, inhabit. So, she must have been wrong."

That softened her up, but she was no dummy.

"OK, sweet talker. Fine. I'll ask Alana myself."

The bar was empty now, except for us and the now sleeping bird. The chairs were up on the tables already, but we had some cleanup behind the bar to finish before we could call it a night.

We worked side by side for another few minutes, playfully bumping our hips together on occasion, apologizing with laughter until I pinned her up against the ice machine.

"I never saw her," I whispered into her ear right after I kissed it tenderly. "I don't think she exists."

~~~

I followed Tatiana's strokes one for one, her paddle on the left, mine on the right. Every ten strokes we switched sides. Sitting behind her I had enough fading moonlight to see the muscles in her back flex and stretch. They performed precisely, directed as fingers on a piano might when creating music.

The cotton deck shorts we both wore covered us but otherwise maintained a comfortable distance away from our awareness. I didn't feel them, yet noticed the drawstrings swayed with our hips as we propelled her outrigger canoe away from shore.

Our breathing was too taxed to talk much, but she hummed a tune that matched the rhythm of our paddling. It felt good to work out again. It had been weeks for me, I could feel my muscles broadcast mild complaints. At the same time, though, they relished the attention.

We were paddling, from what I could tell, straight out to sea. Where she might be taking me was still a mystery. Lanai was several miles away, too far for a casual adventure. As was my habit since arriving back on Earth, I looked up at the stars whenever I got a chance. That's when I noticed the first anomaly.

Although the thin crescent moon looked familiar as it approached the horizon, the stars did not. The Hawaiian 'A'a was directly ahead of us, Sirius as I had learned later in my studies. But, the others were all in the wrong place. The constellations looked slightly elongated as well. Naturally, I tried to figure out what could possibly be wrong with my vision. Perhaps I was tired. Or disoriented some way I hadn't quite recognized.

Finally, Tatiana pulled her paddle from the water. Twisting around she had a sheen of sweat reflecting the ocean's luminescence. Her entire body seemed to be shimmering in the same glow.

"The moon," she pointed at the horizon where it balanced. "She paints a path for us to follow."

"Where are we going, Tatiana?" The star issue was bothering me, despite trying to ignore it.

"We're almost there, I promise."

She turned back toward the front of the outrigger, still holding her paddle out of the water. Mine was resting across my lap when I noticed my second anomaly.

It was turning to dawn.

No way, I figured, had we been paddling for four or five hours. At most it had been fifteen minutes. I turned quickly and looked behind me. Maui wasn't there. Lahaina wasn't shimmering its lights along the shoreline. I turned quickly back to Tatiana to see her raising her paddle in both hands high above her head.

She was chanting softly, almost singing, but my eyes quickly looked just beyond her. There, only a hundred yards in front of us was a magnificent green island, steep peaks rising into a soft purple morning sky, waterfalls gracing each valley and a line of surf surrounding it all.

"How?" I said out loud. I looked all around me, we were surrounded by open ocean everywhere else. I was surely dreaming. Until I smelled the salt spray lightly mingling with some unknown flower fragrance. I had dreamed in color, but never with scents.

Tatiana turned to me again, smiling broadly. Behind her, I could see steep beaches rising up from a lagoon. I heard, but also felt the thunder of the reef breaking apart the sea as it tumbled across.

"Waves," she said. "On empty shores await our arrival."

She turned back to begin paddling.

"What happened to Maui, Tatiana?"

Without turning around, she laughed in celebration.

"We're not there anymore, Hudson."

I looked back one last time. The island of my birth had somehow disappeared. Putting my paddle back into the translucent blue water I moved forward with Tatiana. Toward something that promised more that what was already known. Something wonderful, but special in a way that still hid just beyond a veil of mystery.

"Where are we then?" I asked, needing a verbal confirmation to quell the residual stain of doubt. Old habits and all.

"My dear Hudson, this is Kahiki Nui."

# BEST IN SHOW

Tiwaka's Tiki Bar & Grill was closed Sunday. Not for religious reasons unless you adopted the Old Testament advice that everyone needed one day to rest, even God. We worked our butts off the other six days and really did need what I liked to call a 'mental health day'.

Of course, the cleaning crew we hired came in all day Sunday. And, they needed the entire day to get it done.

I found my way in just before noon. Important things were happening, as evidenced by the two ladies from the Lahaina Farm Fair that were following me. The younger one carried a tablet computer and portable scale. The older one carried a clipboard.

"I appreciate you coming down," I said as I held the back door to the bar open. "Hope you don't mind sneaking in this way. If I open the street side door I'd have to spend an hour flushing curious tourists outside."

The older lady, wearing purple and white, topped with a gold bandanna smiled politely. She wrinkled her nose at the chemical smells coming from the mops in the kitchen, unhappy. The younger one looked interested, having never been 'behind the bar'. She was smiling.

Perspective. It makes all the difference.

"Here you go," I announced proudly. "The best stalk of bananas on the island!"

They both stared in silence.

"Really," I quickly added. "There are thirty hands on this and I'm guessing it weighs at least a hundred pounds."

The younger lady turned away to use an empty table to prepare her scale and boot up her tablet. The older lady, I could tell, was trying hard to suppress her amazement.

"We'll need a moment to document your claim, sir." The older lady was full of formality. Poor thing.

I left them to their devices and went to talk to the cleaning crew. They were some of my favorite people to spend money on. They worked hard, didn't slack off and always impressed me with a spectacular job. Bars can generate a lot of blood, sweat, and tears. Not to mention other bodily fluids, grease spatters and broken glass.

Our restrooms were the cleanest in all of Lahaina, which wasn't saying much, but I still boasted how pristine they were on a daily basis. I always tipped the guys who rotated through that chore. It was something I insisted on. That and the kitchen. We didn't clean the grease traps often, we replaced them. The chimney flume wasn't scrubbed. It was also replaced, every six months.

The bar itself was sterilized, the liquor bottles dusted, the floors serviced by a dozen Roombas every morning. The windows were cleaned, the screens vacuumed.

We did everything right. Why? Because the profits supported it. I could walk into any bar in Lahaina and immediately ascertain which of them was in financial trouble, just by looking at their cleanliness. Sometimes the evidence was glaring. Other times you could see it coming. An owner who was taking too much money out of the business, leaving it to languish. In a year, or two, it would be closed.

Sucked dry by an absentee profiteer. I could care less, except for the employees. Most of them would be knocking on my door soon after, asking for work. Most of them would get turned away. Our staffing was magnificent.

Great pay and benefits. A great boss. A fun and safe place to work. Turnovers usually occurred because of pregnancies, marriages, moves back to the mainland. And half of those made their way back eventually.

Every now and then someone went to jail for something stupid, or got seriously injured surfing, diving or chasing whales in a kayak. But, that was rare.

About as rare as someone winning the Best Banana Award two years in a row.

"Mister Tiwaka," the older lady said, waving her hand for me.

I approached, hands behind my back, trying hard to suppress a smile.

The younger lady was beaming. Her face gave it all away.

"We have measured your stalk of bananas and have found them to qualify for entry into the Lahaina Farm Fair."

She paused.

I took that as my cue to become effusive in my gratitude.

"Really? I'm so stoked! Thank you very much!" I meant every word, of course, but my gestures may have been a bit exaggerated.

"Yes, well," the younger lady began. "We have weighed your entry at 122.5 pounds with a banana count of 300, even." She looked at me with more than a casual interest. "Quite impressive."

Yeah. She was impressed. I could always appreciate a woman who had good taste in men. If she behaved, I might introduce her to Hudson.

"So, Mister Tiwaka," the older lady continued. "Having measured your entry last, we can unofficially tell you now..." she paused and nodded to her younger assistant.

"You have won Best in Show!"

I thought I could see her standing up on her toes slightly.

She was suddenly quite attractive. Probably because she was enthralled with a winner. I would definitely have to introduce her to Hudson now. But, I would have Sandy do it.

# TRIPPING THE LIGHT FANTASTIC

Tatiana guided us expertly through a channel in the reef. Head high waves were roaring on either side of us, peeling with precision across the shallows. Upon reaching the deep waters, where we were, they quietly disappeared, paying deference to my guide.

If I didn't already think I was dreaming, I would tell you that it appeared as if this island was welcoming her. Welcoming her back. The coconut palms lining the beach waved hello. The sea birds swooped in great circles over her head. Small reef fish jumped out of the water just ahead of our outrigger. If I didn't feel like I was tripping I would have thought it unusual to hear them squeak "aloha" on their tiny jumps.

Once inside the reef we entered a lagoon where the water undulated like molten glass, clear and cool, impossibly pristine. The sand just below us matched that just ahead. If was as if the water was truly invisible, only exposing itself with the insistence of light.

Fantastic light. The vibrancy of everything was extraordinary. Shimmering, almost humming with color. The closer we came to the beach, the richer my senses responded. My eyes were seeing colors and textures I had never known were possible. The blues and pastels were familiar. I just never had seen them so... so alive.

Tatiana leaped out of the outrigger as we slid up onto the sand. I climbed out and began pushing from behind, and we soon had it up on the dry sand, and in the shade of a coco. I let my paddle lean against the seat, she let hers cross the railing near the front.

"Welcome, Hudson," she said, smiling at me broadly. "Kahiki Nui, my home away from home." Twirling like a little girl, she giggled out loud, quite unashamed of her youth.

"Kahiki Nui," I repeated. "It's quite lovely…"

She was quite lovely. Tatiana was beaming. In the bar that night we met, she had appeared seductive and beautiful. Now, wearing only paddling shorts and a sheen of exertion, her eyes sparkling like Christmas morning, she was happy. Truly happy. No caveats, no qualifiers. Happy.

Walking toward me, her arms reaching for my shoulders, hugging me, holding my head with her hands, she took a deep breath. I followed, feeling her chest rise and fall. With that embrace, I felt it all fall away. The tension of confusion, the worry about where we actually were, the survival questions that I had been trained to always address with solutions, all dissolved. I felt the weight of time slip away, exposing the kernel of immediacy. Not since I had been a kid had I felt this way.

"Thank you, Hudson," she said softly into my ear. "Thank you for believing in me, for following me here."

I didn't know what to say, except that it was me that should be saying thank you. Like any good man who is lost for words, I found that when a beautiful, half-naked women is hugging you and breathing into your ear, it is always a good idea to kiss her.

She was waiting for me to do so, her lips already parted, her eyes softly watching me approach. Her hands wrapped around my back, caressing the other half of herself.

~~~

We spent the rest of the day loving each other. On the beach, next to a stream, under a small waterfall, in a hammock. Finally, we had to eat. Tatiana showed me her favorite fruit trees, her garden and a spring that fed a large volcanic basin which we drank from. Everywhere around us the island was alive, with birds and plants and a vibration I could only attribute to the 'aina itself, the land, the island.

The light was moving through the jungle trees and vines, bouncing off of it all, leaving a subtle trail of iridescence. The flowers, the trees, the bees all seemed to be saying 'look at me!'.

I did.

Until Tatiana led me to her small cabin several hundred feet up on the slopes of one of the ridges. The view was high enough to see the entire coastline, rounding off on either side, but low enough to hear the surf down below.

"Why don't we relax here and watch the sun set," she offered.

Exhaustion quickly followed her suggestion and sometime later I opened my eyes to find her wrapped in my arms and the stars filling the sky. Stars that were all out of place.

# KUKAHIKO ESTATE

Tiwaka's Tiki Bar & Grill's annual party was always on the third Monday of January. A bar holiday. Being in Lahaina, we always tried to choose someplace new to go and celebrate.

This year we found the perfect spot.

Kukahiko Estate, a family owned oceanfront parcel under the same deed for two hundred years, was perfectly placed behind a lava jetty. The ragged blackness, somewhat bleached by salt and sun defined a beautiful swimming area on one side and a deep ocean entry on the other. It was stunningly beautiful, so much so that dozens of Brides and Grooms spoke their vows in the cool shade of the beach heliotrope trees.

Facing west into the setting tropical sun, the islands of Lanaʻi, Kahoʻolawe, Molokini and the looming mountain range of West Maui embraced a patch of ocean full of whales, porpoises and those humans who enjoyed swimming with them.

The soft, manicured lawn demanded that all shoes be left behind at the house. This grass had been specifically designed, some suspected GMO'd, to gently caress the toes and soles of all who walked upon it.

When the Tiwaka's crew showed up, though, unwelcome shoes were never a problem. Most of them never left the cars and a great deal of them never left home.

I arrived early with the catering folks hired for the day. Everyone had this day off, especially our hard working kitchen staff. As the ice was stacked and the various refrigerators filled I couldn't hold out any further.

The outside was pulling me toward the water.

Out toward the sea, the mythic, radiant, cobalt-blue sea. There, dark blue rolling swells approached that lava jetty after marching across the long depths of the Pacific. Under the shimmering gaze of the day, they churned themselves into a froth of white and light blue. An exuberant saline celebration. Having traveled for days, they crossed the threshold of reef and rock like the winners of a marathon. Every one of them a champion. Splashing, smashing, cheering and thumping the ground at my feet.

This part of the Maui coastline was no less impressive than the landscapes of Tolkien or Heinlein. Here, you could feel the eyes of deep space gazing down upon you. This was a place where the most brilliant hues and textures of the planet proudly boasted their magnificence to the universe. It was a wonder to watch, and I did for hours. I could never really figure out if Kukahiko was showing off to those celestial observers or worshiping them.

Either way, you could feel the love.

Through that soft, manicured lawn.

# FRESH AIR AND BEER

After the big meal was served, after the kids found shade for their naps, just before the adults began snoring not far away, I found some quiet to myself.

Sandy and baby Kiawe were curled up in a hammock, looking more content than the dictionary and all its synonyms could ever describe. Alana and her friends from whatever crazy-fun neighborhood they lived in, were just returning from snorkeling off of kayaks. Those on shore, though, were quickly getting super mellow.

I walked out to the lava jetty, found a spot where I could lean against a not uncomfortable rock, and there... there I could just watch the sea. Just watch. Not analyze, not appreciate. Just watch. And try to not worry. Of course, that wasn't quite possible

Unfortunately, I had not seen Hudson for several days. The hostel where he insisted living had not seen him. Today made five days since anyone had heard from him. I finally had to ask Alana if she had seen that invisible woman friend of his.

She had not.

And, she was none too pleased about it, either. Initially, she wouldn't voice her concern, but when I pressed her she finally relented.

"I told you she was a heart-breaker." Her eyes averted as she spoke this apparently painful truth. Being the idiot that I sometimes am, I asked her why she thought that.

Her answered was guarded, but her affection for Hudson still bubbled forth.

"She's going to take him to places…" she paused and swallowed hard. "Magical places," her eyes caught mine and held them tightly. "Impossible places."

My confused frown was too fast of a reaction. Moments later, though, I figured out that Alana had been to those magical and impossible places already. For better or worse. Her reaction told me she had both enjoyed the experience and missed it terribly.

"Is Hudson safe, Alana?"

She shook her head as if she didn't really know.

"I made it back," she spat on the ground in disgust, then quickly realized what she had done. "Sorry. Yes. He's safe. As safe as any of us are, anyhow."

I fished out another cold beer from my cooler, offered her one and then opened one for myself.

"Alana," I began, trying to measure my words with a dose of compassion tucked nicely inside a shell of curiosity. "Is she, you know, a player?" I drew deep from my beer. On my next breath, before she could answer, I followed up. "Is she using Hudson? You know, he's a bit fragile…"

She held up her hand for me to stop.

"Of course she is. But, in a good way."

Not being as advanced intellectually as most women, I waited for her to simplify that for me. I looked at her, a good deal of blankness in my face. She saw the lack of complete understanding in my eyes, rolled hers and added.

"Her agenda revolves around entertaining herself, to be sure. But, the manner in which she does that is perfectly awesome for those she entertains herself with." She held her hand out for another beer, taking a deep breath of the freshness in the air around us.

I opened it for her.

"I still love her," Alana said quietly. She looked to me to see if I had heard her.

I guess we had crossed over that wall against intimacy that employers and employees enjoy. Both of us squirmed a little inside, where the other couldn't see. However, it was a barrier that had to come down. We both were concerned about Hudson.

My gaze out to sea allowed her some freedom from any hint of judgment or pity. She was an honest human being. We could all be so lucky to have them around us.

The crashing surf replaced our conversation for a full minute or so until I had to ask.

"How long were you gone, Alana?"

She finished her beer and held out for another. As I opened and handed it to her she shook her head, still amazed at the answer.

"Two months."

# HOME MODULE

I felt her stir just before the night acknowledged there was any real hope for dawn. She quietly slipped away as I pretended to sleep. As I listened to her quiet movements, I rolled onto her side of the bed, relishing in her leftover warmth.

There was no really good reason to move out from under the light sheets. The Earth was pulling me toward her with a gently consistent insistence. I wished I could have pulled back as equally. Acquiescence would have to suffice. God, how I had missed gravity.

No straps secured me to a bulkhead. My little slumbering muscle movements didn't throw me up against one constraint or another. I moved nowhere involuntarily. It was as delicious as anything I had ever tasted.

Drifting silently off to sleep again I replayed the days events, like dreams are hell-bent on doing. Except this time there were no surprises. We stripped under the decking on the beach in Lahaina because we had to shed the last remnants of reality. Swimming out to her outrigger canoe did the final cleansing, dissolving any and all fears. Her canoe confirmed we had been properly prepared for things that were quite impossible: this island, the mixed up star fields, a woman so impossibly enticing that I too easily accepted her as my perfect companion. As if it had always been destined for me.

As if life could actually outdo itself to such an extent as to wipe away all memories of tragedy, sadness, fear, boredom and complacency. If that was true, my conscious mind began to wake, I soon realized that yes, it might be possible, but it had never before happened in the entire history of everything.

So how could it be happening now?

"Hudson?" she whispered, pulling the sweet warmness of the sheet off my shoulder. "Are you dreaming?"

I moaned softly. Something close to yes, but not in English.

She sat next to me, her warm thigh sliding up to my arm. Her fingers pushed into my hair, pushing past my ears until it felt like she was cupping my skull with her palm.

Smoothly, her hand twisted my face up to hers.

"Again?"

I rolled over welcoming her as the sheet fell to the floor.

Reality, so I've heard, is highly overrated.

~~~

This went on for what felt like days. Sensual mornings, afternoons in the surf or waterfalls, naps after smoothies, sunset adventures at the beach. And evenings of hedonistic extravagance in a place of few physical possessions.

Finally, I pulled out of my sensory daze enough to ask questions. We were sitting on a cliff edge watching the orange and reds of the setting sun. I think she actually looked amused that it had taken me this long to finally ask.

"Tatiana, if I grow old not knowing where you call home, it would be a terrible shame."

Playfully, she turned toward me, licking the escaping juice of a nearly finished guava from her fingers. There was some hesitation as she searched for an answer.

"Well," she waved her hand across the scene before us. "I call this island Kahiki Nui. It's a moku, you know, an island. Isolated and quite dependent on self-sufficiency."

"This entire island, I mean moku...is this your home?"

"Yes, for now. It's a lot like your Russian module or the European modules in your space station." She sat back on her elbows and crossed her ankles. "But infinitely more comfortable."

I just stared at her, trying to find the analogy she was trying to paint for me. I couldn't. My attention was slowly falling back into a trance.

"Except, I can go where I wish. Anytime. Well, almost." She cuddled up to me, running her open hand up my bare chest. "It is comfortable here, isn't it, Hudson?"

I got the hint. Leaning over to nibble on her ear, I whispered.

"Infinitely."

# HALEAKALA RANCH

We didn't get out of Kukahiko until the next morning.

Darren and Shane had been gracious enough to let us linger. But, there was a wedding scheduled for that evening, so we cleaned up our mess, loaded the vans and backed out of the long driveway.

Tiwaka, who hadn't flown all day, launched from the back of one of the pickups, flew up to a rock outcropping above us and snagged a nearly ripe papaya from a lone tree. Effortlessly continuing to maintain a gentle arc through the crisp morning, Tiwaka glided down toward Darren, dropping the fruit into his outstretched arms. With a squawk and a head nod, he flew back into the truck.

I'm glad he decided to warm up a bit. Where we were going he'd love to fly. Pueo country. The rolling grassy pastures of ranch land climbing steadily behind the coast. Just below the barren lava crown of Haleakala, expansive forests and grasslands filled the flanks. Roads were few, but we had access to a special one leading into the storied expanses of the famed Haleakala Ranch.

~~~

Alana rode with me in the Sprinter van.

At first we just let the small talk fill the spaces. She had climbed in after seeing Sandy and baby Kiawe climb into the motor home to nap. I figured she was making herself available in case I wanted to talk further about Hudson.

I did.

"Glad you jumped in, Alana. Now I can show off my extensive avian recognition skills. There are hundreds of game birds up there, pheasants, partridges, pigeons and even..."

"Peacocks," Alana interrupted. "Any peacocks?"

"Oh yeah," I said, nodding my head knowingly. "They're everywhere." I looked over to her as I made a right turn. "But, I never see any."

Her disappointment felt heavy, right up until the first cattle gate slapped the kitchen dishwasher in the butt as he let it swing shut. After that her mood lightened. Her left hand went back through her hair and she leaned on the window jam, letting the air fill and fluff it further.

I tried to imagine what kind of personality would attract both Alana and my brother. Or, as Alana had hinted, she and Hudson had simply been the unfortunate ones who could see her. Maybe anyone would fall prey to this intoxicating beauty.

I knew all about that.

Sandy was still all that, and more. It might not be scientifically measurable, but I swear she grew more beautiful now that Kiawe was with us. Still, I tried to imagine a woman more captivating, someone with a magnetism that could take a lover for months on end. And, apparently someone who could use that magnetism to bend light and render themselves invisible.

I couldn't.

~~~

The green pastures, decorated occasionally with patches of forest, lay across the land as a carpet, one that had somehow captured and held forever, rolling waters just below.

Quail scurried out of our way as we climbed up the narrow concrete road to the higher and higher elevations. Bleached cow skulls scattered among the kiawe forests in the lower elevations soon got replaced with eucalyptus, waddle and avocado trees. The air had begun with a humid heat and now, at some 3000 feet was blowing Alana's hair back with tree fragrances.

I finally broached the subject.

"Do you know where he might be?"

Alana turned from watching the view to staring at me, anxious to talk about it.

"It's not on Maui," she said suddenly.

"What?" I exclaimed. "Where the hell is he?" Now I was worried. He was supposed to be shacked up in some Lahaina love nest close enough to stumble back to the bar if things went bad. Off island? He had been off planet too long already. Off island was too far away.

"Don't worry, he's still very close." Alana was rubbing her palms along the tops of her legs. Nervousness crawled all over her.

I ran off the road into some gravel, but quickly got back onto the concrete.

"Lana'i?" I asked, relieved that at least I could see the island he might be on. "Molokai?" I added. I could see that island as well.

"No, no, no," Alana said, exasperation in her voice.

That only fueled my frustration. I was about to demand she tell me without all the word games, but she beat me to it.

"He's safe," she said softly. "He's happy. I can promise you that." Quickly, she looked outside again. "Yeah."

I felt my anger slough right off. 'He's happy', she says. Then it might not be any of my business where he was. Except that it was. He was my brother, he was here to recuperate. Maybe he was, recuperating.

"Two months?" I asked.

Alana pulled her bare feet up onto the seat, tucking them up against her thighs. The sun was bathing her skin with a nice warm light, proving she was still quite young.

"It didn't feel like that long," she said. "Maybe a week. I dunno. But, when she had to..." Alana paused to take a deep breath. Like those contagious yawns, I found myself doing the same. "My friends said I had disappeared for two months. Lost my job, my rental, my reputation. Train wreck stuff."

We rolled slowly through another cattle gate, the kitchen guy now having mastered the technique of gate tending.

"Imagine," Alana said, using her hands a bit now. "Going to heaven, thinking this is too perfect to not be forever. And, then finding it's just a... I don't know. A dream?

"It was like I died and then fell out of heaven."

That was heavy. I kept looking over at her, to see if I could find any hints as to her state of mind. Whatever mental breakdown she might have had, Hudson was probably now experiencing. Or not. Maybe they had eaten the same bad mushroom on an old pizza. That prompted my next question.

"So, Alana, how long ago did you, you know, have this experience?" My choice of words sounded a bit unconvinced. I still wasn't a believer in her story.

We were stopped at another cattle gate. I heard her open her door.

"It's all quite real, believe me. When Hudson comes back you can ask him. He's a scientist, maybe you'll believe him over a waitress." She stepped out and closed the door behind her, leaning in the window for a moment. "And, it was over two years ago."

I watched her in my right mirror as she got inside the van behind me. Her hands were moving, fanning flames. My ears were burning.

~~~

Our caravan proceeded up toward the summit. Near the national park entrance of 7000 feet or so, we detoured on a private unpaved road. Moments later we all circled our wagons in a large meadow partially surrounded by pine trees.

Everyone split into whatever groups they usually gravitated toward. That left me by myself. Sandy and baby Kiawe were hanging with the other moms. I hiked up to the ridge facing the rest of the island below us. The view was quite conducive to sorting out drama, like that I was having with Hudson, and Alana.

Experience taught me one thing quite well. If I didn't understand something it didn't mean that something wasn't possible. Only an idiot would assume they knew everything. The perfect analogy was that six hundred years ago the top scientific minds thought the sun revolved around the Earth.

So, how does one get the perspective required to actually begin to understand the things you have grown to disregard. Well, satellites would have helped those Renaissance minds. For me, it was direct observation of people I felt were authentic believers.

Alana was one. Hudson possibly.

Their behavior painted them as knowing something I had yet to learn, or as was usually the case, knowing nothing more than a dream, or theory. A hope.

Alana was confident in her belief that Hudson was in the grasp or control of someone quite a bit more advanced than every other human on the planet. Sure, that was possible. But, I didn't think it true. I thought, unfortunately, that Alana was painfully mistaken, misled or even mentally ill. Hudson was probably on a drunken adventure somewhere. Who could blame him?

Alana said she had disappeared for two months.

I wasn't going to wait for two months to pass before I began searching for Hudson. I would give him two more days, a total of one week, before I sent Tiwaka and the Waikikians on a search and rescue mission.

# UNIFIED FIELD THEORY OF TIKI

Spending a lot of time alone, in space, aboard a relatively small craft lends itself to creative philosophical thought. It wasn't so much the spectacular venue, the view, or the cutting-edge laboratories that inspired such. None of those things contributed like you might imagine.

No.

It was the almost complete lack of interruption.

From what I followed on the Internet while perched high above it all, it appeared that most people in the Western societies were trying to master the art of multitasking. I guess that might be a noble skill to have, but it appeared to never be attainable. What everyone seemed to be actually doing was living a series of linear, short attention slices of time. Similar to how a computer processes multiple tasks, by addressing small slices of their needs, in order, then upon reaching the last one going back to the first and performing the next set of small slices of need.

Unfortunately, none of those thoughts got extended attention. None of them got access to the most powerful analytic computer available. Our own brains.

However, when one has no interruptions, a thought can run for a long while without getting ignored in favor of something new. Multiple options appear as solutions, or numerous directional possibilities appear.

Distractions though were numerous. It had been weeks since I had practiced this technique for problem solving. At the moment, I found myself on the Island of Distractions, in the high favor of her attention starved Queen.

But, there was an issue that had not disappeared with my ignoring it. It returned again and again, every night.

The sky. Specifically, the stars inhabiting that fine place. They were wrong. In the wrong place.

So, I made my way to the beach one early evening, telling Tatiana I wanted a moment to myself. I had to solve this issue with the stars. And, that was impossible while within the reach of Tatiana.

Tatiana knew my background as a scientist, as an astronaut. She felt my confusion, saw it in my eyes every time I looked up. She curled up in bed when I kissed her goodnight. I could see some worry on her face. That, in some perverse way, encouraged me, indicating that my recognition of the star anomaly was not unfounded.

I walked at the water's edge for a while, pacing back and forth down the beach, staring up at the growing darkness. As the veil of space fell up Kahiki Nui, her island, I sat down heavily into the sand.

There it was, I thought. The reason all the constellations looked stretched. Why so many target stars were not in the time-honored relative positions to other stars.

They had traveled quite a way since I had last seen them.

Vega and Canopus were closer together. Beta Centauri and cousin Alpha were skewed, and now that I analyzed each of the stars, and the directions they were moving, relative to Earth, I felt a chill cross my skin.

Still, I couldn't believe my idea. So, I sat there all night, until dawn, locating each star I had studied for decades and applying my theory to its now apparent position in the sky.

When the sky brightened I headed back to Tatiana's cabin. She was still sleeping as I slipped under the sheet next to her. Her warmth was magnetic, drawing me the last few inches across the cool sheets, toward her skin.

I stuck my nose into her hair and somehow thought I might smell something different with her. Different from all other women I had ever met, different from all other women that had ever existed up to this point in time. All I got was jasmine.

Still, I found it extraordinary that she heralded something so intangible while being so damned real. I actually felt pride. For her. For me, in having been lucky enough to meet her. And, finally in the human race. Apparently, we had done better than anyone might have expected.

My arms wrapped around her with an entirely new appreciation.

~~~

We slept a good amount past noon. I might have lasted another couple of hours, but I heard water running in the kitchen. Best alarm clock ever invented.

Tatiana was just turning away from the stove, carrying two platters of steaming breakfast.

"Good morning, night owl," she said.

Her eyebrow was hovering just a bit higher on one side than the other.

"Yeah, about that," I teased. "We need to talk."

She slid the plates onto the round table and turned to get our mango smoothies.

"Well, I know there's no one else on this island, so it can't be that you've found someone else," she laughed. Sitting down, and spreading her napkin across her lap, she bragged. "And, I know it can't be about the food. It's been better than I expected with the equipment I've got."

She reached over and put her hand atop mine.

"But, it might be something else. Yes?"

I nodded, and figured it best to first take a deep drink of the mango cup of courage in my hand.

"Yes," I sat the glass down and licked my lips. "I've got to say, I'm surprised. Proud. Humbled to be sure."

Her eyes playfully tried to hide her acquiescence. The magic was being reduced to science. Reduced to that which can be described. The child in all of us hated that. But, the curious in us relished being able to understand it. She didn't respond, allowing me to tell her more of what I might actually know.

"I figure you must be some sort of historian and maybe even an anthropologist." I put my hand on top of hers now. "Or you may just be a hedonistic young lady who enjoys hanging out with astronauts.

"Don't get me wrong," I reached for my fork. The food was demanding I stop talking and consume it. "I'm honored, but confused."

The first bite was right. I should shut up and chew.

"Hudson..."

"No, seriously. I do love it here. I love you." I stood up. "I love what you are able to do. I want to .." I moved behind her, rubbing her shoulders and kissing her ear. "...know how you do it."

She laughed. Just like your little sister might if she was about to tell you a secret that would blow your mind.

"You already know, Hudson." She turned up to kiss me, whispering right before she enveloped my lips. "You're the inventor."

~~~

"I invent time travel?"

She shook her head no. "Not exactly. Sliding back and forth on a timeline is not possible. Except the relativity way, into the future of someone not moving as fast as you. Even then, you can't go back, and you can't bring anything with you.

"As you can see, I like to travel quite comfortably."

"I can see you do," I spread my arms out. "You bring your own island paradise."

Tatiana offered me some apple she was cutting up.

"Inter-dimensional shift," she beamed. "At least that's what the history books call it."

She reached for another apple. The first was more delicious than I can ever remember enjoying.

"The story goes that you were drinking some concoction in a coconut shell, outside a Tiki bar and the idea came to you. It was, or I mean will be, the missing piece of the Unified Field Theory, specifically that time is not linear. It's a series of dimensional shifts. We move through them as if falling through a gravitational field, thinking it linear when it is actually moving like waves bouncing around inside a sphere.

"Einstein and Hawking got people thinking about curved space, where you might bridge great distances by hopping from one point to another when they got close to each other. But, you, and believe me, I really appreciate your efforts, you proved it is not curved space and distances, but rather waves of complimentary dimensions, each one a tiny slice of time."

My ears were trying to replay what I had just heard. This was good stuff!

She leaned in close and kissed me.

"And, you figured out how to leap from the crest of one wave to the crest of the following one, thereby bridging great distances in time. Yet, we have traveled nowhere geographically."

I had to take a deep breath. Logic was calling. 'Hello, are you home?' It asked. This was crazy talk. Tatiana looked perfectly sane, but the words spilling from those beautiful red lips were far from it.

Insane only because it had no basis in reality. Well, in my reality. The math required to do that kind of theoretical adventuring was beyond me. Besides, there had never been any evidence of anyone traveling back in time from the future. Surely that would have been noticed.

I mentioned that to her.

"Yeah, you're right," she sat back and folded her arms. "I'm the first."

~~~

Before I could ask any more questions, she stood, reached for my hand and led me outside. The grassy area behind her cabin, looking up to a spectacular waterfall in the near distance, was bathed in warm tropical light.

"Do you believe anything I've told you so far?"

Incredulous, I asked, "So far? You mean there's more?"

She shrugged her shoulders. "Yes, a little."

"Well, you're on a roll, keep going!"

She pulled me over to the hammock. I sat down first and she followed up against my hip. Our four feet soon began swinging freely.

"It took a long time to build a machine like this one. A really, really long time, Hudson."

She looked at me as if I might get the point without her having to say it. I guess I might have given enough time.

"OK, OK," she said quickly. "We always talked about this in development, but my theory won them over. You see, Hudson, you invented Inter-Dimensional Shift, but you never got to try it."

Oh, that's not sounding good.

"It was decided that in your honor, the first trip would be back to visit you. To show you the machine and to let you try it. Some said it would taint your eventual discovery, but others said it would motivate you. Others still said it would save you altogether."

"So, I guess you won the contest as the girl that would come back to jump Professor Hudson's bones?"

She laughed like it was 2 A.M. and she had finally figured out I was good-looking enough to sneak in the back door of her fraternity.

"No, although that has been a huge benefit!" She turned away from me, pretending to look at the stove. "OK, maybe some of that is true." She turned and walked up to the wall of the kitchen area, running her hands down the bamboo siding. "I designed this thing. It was the first time anyone ever successfully simulated a machine that could make the shift. Then, of course, it took us ten years to get the parts manufactured, another three to put them together.

"We all had seen the images of you, up in the space station. You're famous, you know."

I think she blushed a little.

"We all wanted to come back to 'jump your bones'. It was a legendary goal of every engineering student, mostly girls, that worked on the project. I insisted it be me when my simulation worked first."

I guess I felt honored if anything. But, I still needed proof. Still needed something to show me that this was all not some tripped out dream. She was watching my face. Suddenly I felt like she might already know what I would think next, having studied it in some cult-like history class.

"If you're the first, then what about Alana, at the bar? She knows who you are."

She blushed again.

"No, she doesn't. She just thinks she's going crazy. I could never tell her what I've told you. You're the inventor! She's..." Tatiana paused. "She's famous as well, but for something entirely different."

"Really, Alana?" I tried to think what would make her famous to people from wherever Tatiana was from. "She can balance four Coco Loco Mocos and six Primo beers on a tray," I volunteered.

Tatiana shook her head, no.

"Not quite, Hudson, although that is an admirable skill to be sure." She reached down to her wrist, where I noticed earlier, she sported a beautifully finished metal bracket.

"It's time we go back to the bar," she turned to face me. "It's time you get to experience Inter-dimensional shift for the second time."

I thought a moment about that.

"The outrigger canoe ride was the first?"

She nodded.

"I want you to hang on, darling."

Closing my eyes, I wrapped my arms around her back, as she leaned her head in and nuzzled my neck. I felt the warm sunshine quickly disappear, replaced immediately by the dim Tiki lights above the dance floor.

"Kiss me, Hudson," she whispered as we soon found our rhythm to the slow song in the background. I didn't want to open my eyes.

Until I felt that damned parrot land on my shoulder.

# SYMBIOTICA

"Hudson!"

The shouts came from so many different directions that I almost didn't notice Tiwaka pulling on my hair with his beak.

Almost.

Alana left her full tray on the bar and ran over, hugging me from behind. The other dancers on the floor turned from their romantic thoughts of monogamy and looked at me, sandwiched between two beautiful women. Some of them smiled.

I could feel Tatiana's hands reach out for Alana. For the briefest of moments they touched, but Alana quickly retreated.

My brother suddenly appeared as well, gently untangling Tiwaka from my hair.

"Nice to see you back, bro." He hugged me, one arm around my shoulder, the other around Tatiana.

"Introductions are in order," he suggested.

Alana leaned in to my brother's ear and whispered a bit too loudly.

"You can see her now?"

Tatiana stepped back, still holding my hand and we all cleared the dance floor. I couldn't help but notice people staring at her. As she moved toward the bar itself, the crowd parted with an almost choreographed cue, everyone turning to watch.

We huddled around the waitress station until two bar stools cleared. Tatiana was gracious, talkative and kept very close to me.

Alana steered clear of her for the most part. I kept looking at her as if I might now be able to figure out why Tatiana had been fascinated with her. Other than her obvious beauty, I came up with nothing.

As the night progressed, and the crowd thinned to those few of us at the bar, I felt I might burst if we didn't discuss why I had been gone and what I had discovered. Just as I was about to bring the subject up, just as the last customers filed out and my brother locked the door behind them, just as Tiwaka settled on his perch next to the vodka, Tatiana beat me to it.

My brother served her up a second Coco Loco Moco and asked, "So, Tatiana, where are you from?"

I felt her nudge me discreetly. She smiled broadly and then turned to him to answer.

"I'm from the future," and quickly pointing to the vodka bottles she added. "And, so is the parrot!"

~~~

I almost laughed when I heard Hudson's girlfriend declare that. Experience and training prevented me from doing so. In a bar, you hear a lot of bat-shit crazy talk. And, I have found that the bat-shit crazy people are very passionate about their opinions. Laughing, with so much alcohol around, was ill-advised.

However, those folks always talked only about themselves. Attention hounds, I suspected. Hudson's girlfriend, Tatiana, had included Tiwaka in her story. That was unusual in the bat-shit crazy world.

Still, I had also seen some incredibly wild things happen, many of them I would have sworn impossible prior to being proved wrong.

But, seriously. Could Tiwaka really be from the future?

I turned and looked at the parrot just in case he might be nodding his head yes.

He was.

But, there was a bowl of chocolate covered peanuts in range and he always bobbed his head when he was working himself up for a foraging mission.

I glanced over at my brother, who was staring at Tatiana with as much surprise as anyone, except maybe Alana. She still had her mouth hanging open.

"So, the future?" I said nonchalantly. "Is that somewhere in Texas?" I knew there were hundreds of strangely named towns in that state.

Tatiana sipped her Coco Loco Moco, but held my eyes with hers. She was enjoying herself with the tease.

No one said anything, and the silence was beginning to embarrass Hudson.

"What she means..." he began.

"2447, approximately," Tatiana said quickly. "Although with some of the relativistic effects, I believe it might be 2449 by now."

Alana moved behind me, putting her hand gently on my back. It felt as if she might actually be using me to help her balance as she moved to my side. Standing shoulder to shoulder with me, and directly across from Tatiana, she leaned over and quietly asked the same question that was foremost in my mind. Well, not the one about her being bat-shit crazy. The other one.

"2447, as in the year two thousand four hundred and forty-seven?"

Tatiana nodded, the Coco Loco Moco straw still connecting her lips to the drink.

"Funny," Alana snorted. "You don't look five hundred years old."

I bumped my hip into Alana's in an attempt to keep her from making this ugly.

Tatiana put her drink down and looked at Alana.

"Could you say that with a little less sarcasm?"

Alana bumped my hip back, all behind the bar and beyond view.

"Well no, then it wouldn't mean the same."

The daggers were flying between these two, and being a good bartender I went into diffuse mode.

"Ladies," I interjected, steering Alana to my other side. "I have a no stink-eye policy after 11 P.M."

Hudson popped out of his trance, or infatuation, or whatever it was that had kept him silent for the last several minutes.

"What do you mean, 'so is the parrot'?" He pointed at Tiwaka. "That parrot? Tiwaka?"

I signaled for the bird by shaking the coconut bowl of chocolate covered peanuts. He had his head completely inside of it within two seconds. I repeated the story of baby Tiwaka for Hudson's girlfriend.

"We found Tiwaka in Haiku, years ago, Tatiana. He was just a young, flightless bird then, his wings cut short by a vet in Honolulu."

Tatiana pushed her empty drink away.

"I know this is a bar, and I realize crazy conversations are typical, especially late at night. But, if you let me talk..."

Hudson interrupted her this time.

"Believe me, guys. I've seen what she can do..."

Alana chimed in at that, still upset.

"You and me both, OK? But, you haven't seen the final act yet, Hudson."

"Alana, please." I raised my hands for a timeout. "Let's let them talk. We can setup a mud wrestling contest later where you ladies can work out your differences."

Tatiana caught Alana's eye at that suggestion, apparently seeing some interest.

"Go ahead," Hudson encouraged. "Tell us about Tiwaka."

"OK," Tatiana glanced once more at Alana, then folded her hands on the bar.

Immediately, we all noticed her bracelet. It played with the light from the Tiki lights in a way I don't think I had ever seen before. It

127

appeared to be a finely brushed metal that was also slightly translucent. Or glowing. Or pulsing. It was a fascinating piece of jewelry. Unique. Like something from the future might be.

"Have you noticed," she began. "How Tiwaka can eat chocolate when no other birds can?"

We all nodded, but remained silent. How did she know this? Perhaps Hudson had mentioned it.

"Have you noticed," she continued. "How Tiwaka understands quite a bit of what you're saying?"

"Sure," I said proudly. "He's a smart bird."

Tatiana watched me and smiled.

"Smarter than you think." She put her hand on Hudson's. "He can understand five spoken human languages and dozens of robotic dialects."

"Robotic?" We all said at the same time.

"I brought him back on my first test trip, dropping him off in the jungle. For his own safety."

Hudson signaled for another Coco Loco Moco.

"Can you make it a double?" He winked. I could see right through that bit of facial theater. He was nervous.

"Wait," Alana piped up again. "Five other languages? Which five?" She turned to look at the parrot, reaching over to smooth his head feathers as he continued feasting on the chocolate covered peanuts.

"English, of course. Spanish, Mandarin, French and..." She paused. "I don't think you have heard of the fifth one yet. Centaurus."

"What?" Again, all of us in unison.

Alana was eager to do battle and turned to Tiwaka.

"Quel jour de la semaine est-ce, Tiwaka?"

He looked up from his nearly empty coconut bowl and thought for a moment. Immediately, he put his head back into the bowl and continued to chase the last few peanuts around.

"See," Alana said. "He doesn't know French!"

"I didn't know *you* knew French," I remarked. Alana. Wow. What a modern girl of mystery and intrigue!

Just then Tiwaka started stomping his right foot. Once, twice, three times, four.

Tatiana smiled.

"Today is Wednesday," Hudson said. "Day four of the week?"

That was slightly impressive, but we had seen the parrot perform many an amazing feat. Understanding French was new, but not proof of him being from the future. However, the chocolate thing had garnered many a complaint over the years from bird lovers, all of whom accused me of putting poor Tiwaka in harms way.

"What about the chocolate addiction?" I asked.

Tatiana got up from her bar stool, pushed it back out of her way and leaned on the bar. Alana moved behind me quickly, again standing directly across from her nemesis.

"You never even said goodbye!" Alana cried. "Not a word! You take me to heaven," her sobs interrupted her for a brief moment. "And, then you drop me in purgatory and leave!"

Alana moved back from the bar and into the rack of clean glasses just behind her. Before anything fell down, she took a step forward. I sat back down, once I saw that the glassware was safe.

Hesitation marked Alana's face between the tears. She stood there, as stoically as possible, waiting for an explanation.

Hudson's face was falling into a frown, he continued looking between Tatiana and Alana.

Awkward.

"I wouldn't exactly call this purgatory," my voice trailing off in mock insult.

Alana didn't find it funny and turned to leave.

"Alana," Tatiana said softly. "That was over a year ago, for you. It was five for me. I'm sorry. Time moves differently for you and me." She reached for Alana's hand but couldn't reach. I pushed Alana forward slightly until she was within range.

Peacemaker is my middle name.

"You're special, Alana," Tatiana said with, I'm sure, every ounce of honesty she possessed. I just wasn't sure how much she carried around with her.

I could see Hudson squirming now as Tatiana held Alana's hand.

"Alana, you are one of only two people someone from five hundred years in the future would come back to see." While that was sinking in, she put her hand behind Hudson's head and pulled him in closer to kiss. She still held Alana's hand as she did.

"Hudson," Tatiana said, smiling. "Is the other one."

Alana pulled away from the kissing couple and walked back behind me and around to where Tiwaka was sitting.

"That's cool. I'm over it," she said, trying to hold her head high. "I've never been that good with sharing."

Stroking Tiwaka's feathers, she picked up the conversation where she had interrupted it.

"What about Tiwaka and the chocolate?"

Tatiana embraced the compromise with a friendly nod. She took a deep breath and began the story.

"Tiwaka is one of the last of his kind, the tropical birds. Genetic engineering, which started in your time, progressed spectacularly by the time Tiwaka hatched. However, there were occasional problems. A corn variant developed by the descendant of your Monsanto Corporation released a gene that when paired with the common cold virus began to infect the world's macaws and related birds. Two dozen species began dying off in the millions. Once it was discovered it was debated for years. Stop the corn and save a few birds or feed the world? You might guess how that debate went.

"Immediately, the genetic engineering was directed at protecting these birds. That had always been the argument for approval of GMO industries: if we have an accident, we know how to fix it.

"Most of the tropical species had initially taken well to the GMO engineering that protected them. There were minor side effects. One of them was the ability to process the enzymes in chocolate, something they had never had before."

Tiwaka spread his wings wide and began parading down the length of the bar.

"Nine months after we thought we had the birds protected the new variant virus morphed into something more dangerous. Fast and deadly. The vulnerable bird species went from exposure to death in as little as twenty-four hours. Thousands of birds were dying each month. So, one of our first proofs that we could even do this kind of travel was to send Tiwaka back, to save him."

The proud parrot was spinning slowly and flapping his wings as if flexing impressive muscles, broadcasting to all who would gaze upon his magnificence that he was indeed awesome.

"And," Tatiana added. "I can see it worked quite well."

~~~

I ignored the clock's impossible opinion that it was 4:20 in the morning. Everyone seated at the bar were looking strong enough to make it until dawn. Tiwaka was the only exception, already perched on his koa swing, feathered head leaning against one of the sides, sleeping. Somehow, he managed to keep a little back-and-forth going all night. Is that something they did in the future? I'd ask him tomorrow, in French!

I watched him sleep while the others continued talking about all kinds of crazy stuff. His feathers looked like a nice colorful blanket he had pulled up around himself during a cool evening. His beak, although slightly blemished with a few scratches occasionally opened slightly, as if he was taking a deep breath. He had been my best friend since I was a kid, had helped me bury old Ococ, had rescued the street performing parrots of Waikiki and now helped provide fresh fish to all the restaurants in Lahaina.

But, I digress. You already know the parrot is amazing.

~~~

"Symbiotica," Tatiana repeated.

"You guys renamed Earth? To Symbi…symbi whataca?" Alana was incredulous.

"Symbiotica."

Poor Alana was shaking her head. Somewhere inside her head the stress must have eaten through that last bit of protective layer between pain and scarring.

"Wait," Hudson held up his hands. "You mean that it's like calling the Earth Gaia or Mother?"

Tatiana pushed her bottom lip out for enough time to weigh the question properly.

"Not like that. The World Governance Council voted and it passed. All countries use the new name, everyone can pronounce it." Tatiana looked around to everyone along the bar. "Isn't it beautiful? Sym-bi-otica! Rolls right off your tongue, after first having a visit with your heart."

"Yeah, but what does it mean?" I looked to the end of the bar and noticed someone in the shadows. The overly tanned tourist lady from last week. She was super dark now.

"Symbiotic relationships are those defining a mutually beneficial arrangement between two, or more organisms," Tatiana explained. She could immediately see in our eyes that a more effective way to tell us would be with examples. "The human body is not entirely human. You know that. We have a cornucopia of other organisms living in our gut, for example. Without them we would be dead in a month. Naturally, without us these various species would also be in danger of extinction. Mites, so small we can't see them, crawl all over our skin, eating and disposing of our own discarded cells. We feed them well and they always clean up after themselves.

"Symbiotic examples are prevalent throughout nature, but more so here..." she paused. "On Earth."

I put a chilled mug of rainwater in front of her. She sipped it a moment, and continued.

"Our oxygen comes from the ocean's plankton, for the most part. Your food from the soil, your energy, ultimately, from the local star. "Yet..." she shook her head. "Yet, the pollution your century's societies poured into the sewer you call an ecosystem took us two centuries to clean up.

"A lot of things died.

"Earth isn't just another planet among countless others with intelligent life, but it also happens to be the most densely populated collection of symbiotic energy in the known universe."

Tiwaka began snoring, on cue according to the opinions of a few in the bar. Tatiana got the hint. This was the short-attention-span century. Silly girl. Everyone knew that.

Hudson leaned in close.

"Got anything for breakfast?"

Of course I did!

It was the last thing the chef and cooks did before they went home at night. Stock one of the refrigerators with some midnight snacks, which was mandated to include waffle dough. Already mixed with blueberries and mashed walnuts.

"But, enough about all that," Tatiana said softly.

"Why were you invisible to everyone earlier? Only Hudson and I could see you. What was that all about?" Alana was getting her second wind.

"If I tell you, you will all just shake your heads in disbelief. I realize my story thus far is so impossibly outrageous that you really don't believe I'm from five hundred years in the future. You also don't really believe that your parrot friend, Tiwaka, is as well, or that he was sent back to protect him from a deadly bird virus.

"You also won't believe it when I tell you that the most famous people of the Twenty-first century are right here in this bar. Furthermore," Tatiana said, standing again. "You would never accept the fact that the first person to live to be five hundred years old is alive right now."

She waited a moment as we had to accommodate the weight of what she had just said. I tried doing that with a quick sip of the already opened bourbon.

"And, that person is also in the bar right now."

I laughed at that, unable to restrain myself.

"What the heck does a five hundred year old person look like?"

Tatiana smiled and looked along the bar, catching all of our eyes.

"Ugly, to be honest. But, she is absolutely gorgeous at this exact moment." Tatiana walked up to Alana, holding out her hand. "I'm sorry I treated you like I did. I lost track of my mission, failed miserably on that first try." Tatiana brought Alana's hand up to her lips. "You are that spectacular."

"Alana?" I asked. "She's going to live to be five hundred?"

"One of most amazing stories we study in school. Alana, my friends, is just getting started, here in your little beach side Tiki bar." Tatiana kissed her on the cheek.

Alana melted right there. In front of everyone. We had to scoop her up with mops and sponges, squeeze her into a bucket, stir, no shaking please, and put her back on her feet.

"You," Alana said under her breath. "Are unfairly dangerous."

Tatiana nodded acknowledgment.

"Sorry," the girl from the future admitted. "I'm only human."

Turning quickly on her feet, Tatiana approached Hudson, wrapping her arms around him and squeezing him tightly.

"Oh, Hudson. Thank you so very, very much."

He looked at her, head cocked slightly to the side.

"What for? Being a living history lesson that entertained you on your private yacht-island?

"Don't get me wrong," he quickly added. "I'm good with that."

Tatiana didn't answer his question. Why bother fabricating a lie to deny it. Why answer it if you were forced to admit it, or lie. A small, innocent smile would have to be all they got.

"You never answered my question, about why only Hudson and I could see you earlier. Now, apparently, everyone has the pleasure."

Tatiana visibly flinched as the barbs took hold.

It was unfair, we could all see that. Alana was a jilted soul, a bad start to the next four hundred and seventy something years.

"This Inter-Dimensional Shift I use to travel like this takes advantage of that wonderful piece of intuitive thought Hudson, the inventor, saw.

"Funny, how you used to call it a Unified Theory, before Hudson came up with his revolutionary theories, when it was obvious there were different physics for each dimension. Namely, the vibrational ranges of matter. Everything else is the same. One of those differences can be manipulated to let visible light bounce off me, where you can then see me, or, pass right through me, making me invisible.

"Hudson and Alana, and this is the part where I expect you'll throw your arms up in complete exhaustion, are special in yet another way."

We all looked at the two of them a bit more closely. Nothing, I got nothing.

"They are the first two known examples of an amazing evolutionary mutation everyone now has, in the future."

I checked Hudson again, studying his hair, his arms, his face. Nothing. I saw nothing mutating.

"Somehow, these two late twentieth century babies managed to have an existing gene turned off, allowing them to see different vibrational energies. Some geneticists theorize it was an epigenetic event, triggered by lifestyle, experience or food poisoning. Well, maybe not the last one."

Alana, as I swung my heavier and heavier head to look, stood stoically, arms crossed, chin thrust forward, feet slightly apart as if she might strike a boxing pose at any moment.

Tatiana continued, touching her bracelet.

"I can broadcast a skin tight, very low energy field from here. It allows me to adjust for different dimensions, as needed."

That's when my crazy detector started going into high alert. It usually gets warmed up when people start saying stuff you know they can't prove. My patience and ability to stay up all night had its limits.

It was the crack of dawn and I had to work again tonight.

"Kids," I said to everyone. "Use the back door, please. I'm off for a nap, big day and all." I walked up to Hudson. "Good to have you back." I put my arm on Tatiana's shoulder, just so I could say I had actually touched a person from the future. "Take care of my brother. Nice to meet you, Tatiana."

I quickly exited into the kitchen, opened the door into my small office, pulled the futon from the closet and let it fall to the floor. I was right behind it a moment later.

# IS THE SKY SAD BECAUSE IT'S BLUE?

I spent the next two weeks with Sandy and baby Kiawe, and Tiwaka, down at the Lahaina Banyan Tree Flight School and Fishspotting Collective. Or so they called it. My stay-cation suited me just fine. The bar was in good hands and I had to assume my brother was too.

He had disappeared again.

Sandy tried to distract me from the worry that must have been written all over my face. All over my attitude. Baby Kiawe, just beginning to walk, stumble and laugh about it was super entertaining. Sandy orchestrated the shave ice, the lunches, and the stolen kisses.

Ma and Pa drove out from the jungle, bringing mangos, papayas, and more bananas. I never told them much about Tatiana other than she was a beautiful woman who had captured Hudson's attention completely. Pa nodded, accepting the explanation without question. Ma wanted all the details. I think Sandy filled her in a little, but I had asked her to not mention the time travel stuff. That would just worry them.

We already feared for Hudson's mental health, as did NASA, and a story about a time-traveling, or inter-dimensional shifting lover would only make things more complicated.

My family did what we did best. We ignored the negative aspects of a problem but worried about the lack of positive ones.

There was plenty of negative surrounding Hudson. He was on indefinite leave from his employer, he insisted on living in a hostel and his infatuation with Tatiana looked to be too consuming. Maybe those weren't all that negative. But, if I let my mind wander it took me to scenarios like: what does an unemployed Ph.D. in Molecular Astrophysics, living with transients do when his bat-shit crazy girlfriend says she wants to time travel?

I guess he would go.

From my perspective, stuck quite firmly in the present, I could see few positives of a time traveling girlfriend. Alana had an opinion on this as well. For the sake of argument, I let my thoughts consider the ramifications if Tatiana could indeed do what she said she was already doing.

She had come back to meet two important people in her history, and get to know them quite intimately. Where would she go next? Who else in the vast timeline of fascinating people would she want to also hook up with? Anthropology had never seemed interesting to me, until now.

Baby Kiawe was on all fours after a falter in his balance. Sandy was encouraging him to continue toward her, across the lush green grass, by jumping up and down and cheering.

One thing I could intuit without a scientific background was this – time travelers would never stay in one place. Even one as amazing as this one.

~~~

Alana was worried more than anyone.

After almost two weeks of Hudson being absent she finally approached me. She found me napping in my hammock behind the bar, under the avocado tree. It was between seasons. My first night back was only hours away.

I don't know how long she was standing next to me while I slept. Hopefully, not long enough to see me drool in my sleep. She finally pushed the hammock enough to begin a subtle swing.

I opened one eye.

"Good afternoon, boss!"

I opened the other eye. Only because I had to.

"Yes, Alana?" I didn't attempt to hide all of my irritation at being woken, just some of it. She didn't care.

"Have you seen Hudson?"

I hadn't, and she knew it. This was just her way of opening a conversation.

"He's still with Tatiana, I assume." I reluctantly swung my legs out of the hammock and sat up.

"Look," Alana continued, trying to contain herself. "I did the math..."

That caught me off guard, unfortunately it showed.

"Hey, don't be so surprised," Alana complained, with a smile. "It was only addition."

"OK, what?"

Alana shifted her weight to her other hip in preparation of explaining her numerical discovery. Her stance relaxed as she began moving her hands to explain.

"I counted the days from when I met Tatiana until she dumped me..."

"Alana," I interrupted. "Who does that?"

"Yeah, well," she ignored the implication. "I do. Anyhow, today is that same number of days. For Hudson."

"So, you've been counting the days since Hudson met Tatiana? Alana, I think that's a bit obsessive, don't you?"

"No, silly! I haven't been counting the days. I only just now counted them. I was having my morning kale smoothie out by the lighthouse and it just popped into my mind. You know, to check."

I shook my head in disbelief.

"Anyhow," she continued. "Today is the day we'll see Hudson."

I got out of the hammock and stood out where the sun could warm me a little and possibly sterilize some of the crazy that Alana was throwing at me.

"She told me once, when she let her guard down," she smirked, as if proud of some unmentionable talent she had in getting time travelers to confess their secrets. "Her power source wasn't infinite. She had to return to her time, or dimension or wherever and refuel."

I nodded just to keep this conversation as short as possible. Extending it by asking logical questions would do nothing constructive.

"She left me that same day."

"Look, Alana," I began, trying to find the best words to express my waning interest in her lost love.

She held up her hands for me to stop.

"I only bring this up because Hudson's your brother. OK? He's going to need your help."

I re-engaged.

"What kind of help?" Now she had me worried again.

"He's going to be very depressed."

We both looked at each other for several moments. I, lost in my thoughts about poor Hudson, and Alana watching for my reaction. She apparently didn't believe she had sold me yet on the seriousness of the problem.

"I thought about suicide when she left me. It was scary. I went to a psychologist who finally did a drug screening. We eventually found out that it was a depression brought on by the lack of whatever drug she had intoxicated me with.

"I was in withdrawal, detox."

"She drugged you?" I asked, incredulous about this new information. "You think she's drugged Hudson too?"

Alana was tearing up.

"How?" I yelled. That only made Alana start crying more. She put her hands up to her face, trying to contain what couldn't be contained.

"How, Alana? How did she drug my brother?"

Taking a difficult deep breath, she wiped her cheeks.

"She only needs to touch you."

~~~

I couldn't concentrate on my work at the bar. I poured so many out-of-whack drinks that someone thought I was inventing new ones. Sandy pulled me off to the side during a lull in the action. I didn't even try to hide my anxiety.

"What's wrong, baby?"

I steered her into a corner of the kitchen where no one could hear us.

"This girlfriend of Hudson's, Alana's ex, you know, Future Girl?"

Sandy knew who I was talking about without the genealogy.

"Well, I know this sounds crazy. I guess Alana is getting to me. Anyhow, I guess it's kind of possible, but she's not what she seems, Sandy. Not at all."

"I know, honey. She's just some cute young thing that likes to tell stories. You know, like yourself. Harmless entertainment."

"No! Sandy, Alana says..."

"Wait," Sandy interrupted. "Alana is a jilted lover. She'll say anything to discredit Tatiana, Future Girl, whatever you want to call her. Don't let anything she says bother you. OK?"

Her logic comforted me for a moment. But it passed quickly. I felt the anxiety fill me up again.

"Sandy, what if it's true? What is Future Girl is some hedonistic time traveler whose real mission is to drug ancient peoples and have sex with them?"

Sandy put one hand on her hip and let her eyebrows lower in disgust.

"Seriously? Is that what Alana says?"

Sandy spun around and looked away from me. I knew that tactic. She was hiding an ugly face twisted by a rising anger.

"I'm going to talk to Alana right now!"

Sandy stormed off, cornered Alana by the women's restroom and a few moments later returned.

"Well, that may have backfired a bit," Sandy said sheepishly.

"Why?" I looked toward the entrance. Alana had her purse and was walking out. "She's going home?"

"No," Sandy murmured. "She quit."

~~~

I spent the next morning at a little beach north of Lahaina, at the beginning of the Ka'anapali resort. The sun always painted this side of the island with special shades of soft blues, all of which would quickly be lost to the glare of mid day.

Above me, the sky seemed so patient. It painted our world with a beauty we seemed to ignore most of the time. Our drama, our manufactured distractions, our lustful motivations were all non-consequential to this tolerant overlord.

Yet, as I watched it closely, I could sense its disappointment at times. Perhaps it was more of a sadness. A sorrow in witnessing the continuous repeat of mistake after mistake by those it cared for, down below.

I got up to walk back to Front Street.

The sidewalk ran ahead of my measured steps as I took my time retreating to reality. I looked up one more time.

Despite what most of the tourists would feel today, I knew that at some level, the sky was blue for an entirely different reason than they thought.

~~~

I got back to the bar earlier than I had planned. With all that extra time I made my way to the hammock under the avocado tree. It just seemed to be the most logical way to spend an extra hour, or two.

Yet, I hadn't been asleep for more than half a dream before I felt the hammock being gently pushed.

I opened one eye.

"He's back," Alana said, a great big grin practically pulling her face to both sides.

I opened the other eye. He was standing next to her.

"Hudson!" I said enthusiastically. "Good morning!"

I quickly got up and hugged him. That's when I felt the tremors in his body, the sobs. Alana's eyes found mine. They were silently saying 'I told you so'.

"What's the matter, bro?" I pulled myself back but held onto his shoulders. He looked completely devastated.

Hudson just shook his head and looked down to his feet, to the dirt below his slippers and the crushed avocado leaves, all checking his descent any further into the dark depths.

"Hudson and I had a long talk this morning," Alana said softly, her hand gently resting on Hudson's shoulder. "We've got our own support group now."

I saw right through that immediately. Alana, who had been crushing on my brother from day one now had a kindred soul. One she could perhaps adopt, or at least love.

But, that was too cynical a thought to hold on for any longer than it took to banish it from my mind.

"Hudson," I said quietly. "Are you OK?" He shook his head no. "Are you hurt anywhere?"

He made a fist and pounded the center of his chest.

Of course.

"Any blood?" I tried to clarify my concern. Standard paramedic questioning. Don't let the emotional shock of a patient distract you from checking for physical damage.

"I checked him out already," Alana said, stepping slightly between Hudson and I. "He's got all his extremities."

Wow, I thought. She didn't waste any time.

Hudson moved to my hammock, lay back and covered his face with his hands. I could see tears sneaking past and sliding down to his neck.

"Hudson?" Alana moaned. "You'll be OK, I promise." Her hand gently caressed his hair. "In a while."

~~~

Hudson moved in with Sandy, Kiawe and I the next day. He did little more than sleep late and go to bed early. He did help with the dishes, though.

At his request, Alana and I went to the hostel to retrieve his things. It required a long drive to Wailuku, giving us a good chance to talk. Or not.

I was getting a bit tired of all the drama, especially with Alana. She was always in the middle of a mess of some kind, nothing disastrous mind you. Just unnecessarily problematic. 'Dramatic, no fire.', a favorite term of my Italian friend Dario Benvenuti described her perfectly. That was Alana.

We were approaching Maui's only car tunnel while climbing the pali on our way to town.

"Will you please honk the horn?" she asked.

I quickly glanced at her. This was stuff we did with kids. I glanced at her again. She was still just a kid.

I honked the horn all the way through the tunnel. Others going the other direction were doing so as well. When we exited I could hear her giggling.

"Thank you," she said. After a moment, she looked out toward the ocean below us, to her right. "Just like old times."

I stole one more glance at her childlike appreciation of something so simple, something that took no effort or cost a penny. Right there, going forty-five miles per hour, swinging through the curves and dodging tour buses I felt my irritation with her melt away.

Silently, I wondered if she would retain that same joie de vie for the next four centuries.

~~~

The nice people at the hostel needed to confirm Hudson's approval before we could remove his possessions. Finally, Sandy got him on the phone, he gave them the secret password or whatever it was they needed, and we were allowed into his room.

Alana seemed a bit shocked.

I had seen worse, but only in the movies.

The place was barren. Only a mattress on a dusty floor separated the room from complete emptiness. A backpack sat atop the mattress. A rumpled sheet was bunched up at one end.

No lamps, no refrigerator, no chair. Nothing but a place for desolate souls to sleep.

I grabbed the backpack and we left as quickly as we could.

~~~

Several days later Hudson's NASA arranged appointment with a psychologist finally arrived.

We both sat silently in the holding room. The waits were apparently so long that DVD players had long ago replaced old magazines.

After forty-five minutes, an excited older gentlemen wearing a sweater and holding an unlit tobacco pipe rushed into the room from the hallway behind the receptionist.

A young lady was following him, holding a clipboard.

"Hudson? Is there a Mr. Hudson here?"

We both stood up.

The older gentlemen rushed over and reached for my hand, shaking it vigorously.

"I am so honored to meet an astronaut!"

"Sorry, sir. Let me introduce you to my brother, the astronaut."

He turned to Hudson and forced back a frown.

"Ah, then. Mr. Hudson," he said with noticeably less excitement. "Well, follow me."

My brother didn't fit the part I guess. It might have been the hair in need of a cut, the hobo beard and the surf trucks hanging as loosely off his frame as the 'Maui Wowee' t-shirt.

I suppose, with my clean cut looks I presented less of a challenge. Hudson, I'm sure, was broadcasting to any and all psychologists a look of desperation and unsolvable mysteries.

As they walked away, I fell back into the almost comfortable chair I had previously warmed up, found a new movie to watch and wasted a few more hours.

~~~

On the ride back to Lahaina, Hudson was still quiet as we approached the tunnel.

"Alana likes it when I honk the horn," I offered. The radio stations were doing little to break the tension.

He only nodded.

I didn't honk the horn.

Finally, near the first beach, he opened up a bit.

"NASA wants me back."

I almost pulled the car over and hugged him.

"Wow, Hudson! That's great news!" After a moment, and only because I was his brother would I ever ask, "So, the psych evaluation went well then?"

There, I saw it, finally. A smile on a face trying to surface from just under the water.

"I've always said NASA wants well-adjusted people to go into space. What they really get are smart people who can fake it."

"So, that psychologist back there warmed up to you, then?"

Hudson laughed out loud and looked at me.

"Yeah, he wants to play golf next Tuesday."

We drove past multiple road side beaches, each filling with parked cars, trucks and pitched tents. Fishing poles filled the areas between groups of body boarders and swimmers. Hundreds of people were out enjoying the sunshine.

I glanced up at the blue sky. It was looking a little blissful.

# NEST OF DREAMERS

Alana met us behind the bar.

Running to Hudson, she practically knocked him over as she squeezed all the worry out of herself, and the air out of him.

"Hudson!" She sang. "You look so much better!"

"You're looking pretty good yourself, Alana!" He hugged her back and if I wasn't mistaken, kissed her on the cheek. "Thanks for helping me out."

Alana glanced back at me as they held their embrace. I got the hint and turned back to retrieve Hudson's backpack for him. Through the window of the car, I watched her capture his face with her hands, guiding him for a long kiss.

Part of the therapy, I figured.

After the appropriate amount of time hiding in the car, I made some noise getting out and walked toward my office.

"Your backpack will be in my office," I said as I walked in the back door. If Hudson needed to escape he would have taken that opportunity.

He didn't.

I sat his backpack in my computer chair and quickly went to my little window facing my car. They were already in the hammock, writhing like a couple of snakes.

The two most famous people of the Twenty-first century were making out in my hammock. I tried to feel honored.

~~~

With all of Hudson's recent issues, I found one of my long suppressed bad habits, or maybe it was only a weakness, surfacing. I felt compelled to protect him. Not just by deflecting rude people or predatory women, although I might be failing in that at this moment, but quite beyond what would be considered common decency.

For instance, here I was, in the privacy of my office, while Hudson was engaged with other matters, and I wanted to go through his backpack. What if someone at the hostel had planted something on him, for whatever reason, and that somehow surfaced. It would kill his NASA gig, embarrass our parents and begin a possibly long list of bad things.

I only wanted to help.

Checking the hammock again, which I shouldn't have done, because there are some things you just can't un-see, I sat back down. The backpack was in my lap, silently asking if I really wanted to do what it thought I wanted to do.

I didn't. But, I would.

I unzipped the main compartment and peeked inside. Nothing unusual. A Ziploc of dirty clothes, a toiletry kit and on the side, a book. I pulled the book out.

UNIFIED FIELD THEORY for DUMMIES, by K.C. Ocaepe.

My heart was racing now. Tatiana had ranted something about Hudson improving this scientific idea. Maybe it had made him curious, I thought. That must be it.

I rifled through the rest of that compartment, just to be sure. Like a TSA guy at the airport would. I put everything back but didn't add the brochure the government usually did.

There were three side pockets, bulging with mysteries.

Standing up, but not wanting to look, I checked on the status of the hammock crew. Alana was topless now, sitting on top of Hudson.

I'm glad they were both over Tatiana now.

The first side pocket held his wallet with one debit card, $320 in cash and a Florida drivers license. Oh, and his NASA photo ID. He looked a lot younger in the picture.

No drugs, no weapons. This was a good sign.

The second pocket held a Maui bus schedule, being what it was, it occupied one side of one piece of paper. A package of Kleenex kept it company. I'd cry too if I had to wait an hour for a bus.

Finally, the last zipped up pocket opened to my view. I reached in and felt around. A soft cloth, similar to what you would clean a camera lenses with greeted me. Just underneath was something metallic. My imagination immediately thought weapon. A small gun or a folding knife. All kinds of horrible scenarios paraded across my consciousness before I could tell them to shut up.

I pulled whatever it was out of the pocket, still wrapped in the soft camera cloth.

Alana was laughing loudly out in the hammock. I didn't have much time.

Unfolding the cloth, I felt my heart sink. In an instant my manufactured little world of Tiki, surfing, family and all other things that so convincingly painted my well structured idea of reality, collapsed.

He had a bracelet just like the one Tatiana had been wearing, except this one was a different color. And, it was humming.

~~~

I put Hudson's backpack under my desk and walked into the bar. I didn't know what to do with myself. How could any of that woman's story possibly be true? I had spent a lot of mental energy invalidating all of her stories. There was an explanation for every thing she had said. Hudson had not been kidnapped by a time-traveling, nymphomaniac from the future. No way.

It was all just a story to keep things interesting in a small harbor town nestled against some mountains of an island in the middle of a very large ocean. Sometimes one had to invent things to keep it fresh around here. Tatiana, in my opinion, and Alana to some degree had special gifts for doing so. They might even be convinced their own stories were true. A little crazy didn't hurt most people. Functionally crazy. I'd seen it many times.

But, that bracelet! It wasn't something that anyone was making, anywhere on this planet. It was too spectacular a piece of technology to have not heard of it. The way it bent light was unique. The brushed metal that allowed light to penetrate beyond the surface reminded me of curly koa wood, giving it a three dimensional aspect.

Hudson had told me how she always wore it. On the mythical island she had taken him to, swimming in the sea, making love. Always. Now he had one.

But, at least he wasn't wearing it.

~~~

Sandy and a new bartender trainee showed up early. I needed a break, mostly to talk with Hudson about the bracelet. Of course, he would know I had invaded his privacy. I would frame that offense with my concern for his well-being. It didn't make it right, it only explained why.

Alana and Hudson finally came in from their afternoon delight, all smiles and quite thirsty. As Sandy and her trainee washed up and got behind the bar, I finished up three smoothies.

"I thought she quit," Sandy whispered

"She's here with Hudson, not to work. I think."

I needed to get Hudson away from Alana for a moment. When Sandy took a moment to talk with her, apologizing for getting angry the other night, I guided Hudson outside.

"Feeling better?" I teased.

"Oh yeah," Hudson grinned.

The afternoon crowds in Lahaina were waning a bit as most people went back to their hotels, or cruise ships to shower from the day's adventures and prepare for the evening ones.

"Look, Hudson," I began. "I need to ask you something. I'm not sure why. I just have to."

He looked at me for a moment. A long moment filled with suspicion.

"OK, what?"

I paused at the edge of a cliff of trust I was about to jump off of.

"Your backpack. I saw the bracelet."

"What!" Hudson yelled. "What were..."

He grabbed my shoulders with both hands.

"You didn't put it on did you?"

"Of course not..."

"Good," he relaxed a bit. "Don't."

He let me go and turned to absentmindedly watch a group of bicycles ride by.

"Don't ever!" he repeated to me.

"Hudson, OK, I got it. Why don't we sit down and you explain a few things to me."

We crossed the street. There we sat on the sea wall, watching the little sailboats dance in front of the island of Lana'i, far enough away to not care.

"You weren't supposed to see that," Hudson said. "What the hell were you doing in my bag anyhow?"

"It wasn't right. It was just that when we went to the hostel, the place looked sketchy. When you told me NASA had called you back, I had visions of some hobo at the hostel putting contraband in your bag."

"What, are you kidding?"

"I know! I know! Stupid sequence of events. I was just looking out for you. You've been in space for a long time. I've been down here a long time, with the riffraff."

Hudson didn't say anything again. One of his long silences that I was getting accustomed to. Finally, after an obnoxious bus passed behind us he turned and looked at me. Seriousness all over his face, like a bad sunburn.

"Look, I realize no one believes the whole Tatiana time-traveling story. I get it. I really do. But, there are somethings about her, about that story, that whether you believe it or not, must remain secret.

"For instance, that bracelet. It's very dangerous, bro. Tatiana told me how in the beginning of their Inter-dimensional Shift testing several dozen people decided to run off and try it. Be the first out of the gate. You know. Happens every day. Not always successful.

"None of them returned. None. No one knows why, but we do know one thing. A meeting had been held with everyone involved, before the final beta versions were finalized. They talked about what would happen if these devices didn't work bi-directionally. You know, one way tickets only.

"Obviously now, Tatiana and I suppose others like her, have that figured out. She said it was not always that way.

"Anyhow, this meeting, where they were talking about what-if this and what-if that, a novel idea was discussed. How to leave a message. For the future.

"For instance, if you went back in time, got stuck and couldn't return, how would you let your future contemporaries know what happened to you?"

"There were really discussions about that?" I asked.

"I guess so. Makes sense. We've had talks at NASA about a plan to initiate if some alien intelligence shows up on the Space Station."

"Really? That's pretty cool," I loved this stuff.

"Yeah, as long as they're nice aliens. With all the rotten humans we have it's safe to assume there are plenty of rotten aliens too."

"Anyhow," Hudson continued. "They decided at this meeting on a system of hieroglyphics that might be used, or introduced to the people native to that timeframe. I mean, if you're stuck in the Egyptian pyramid-building days, you can't exactly be carving stones with "Kilroy was here."

I laughed at that. Imagine some mummified tomb was opened and that phrase greeted you at the door. My mind was enjoying that visual as a hobo type walked along the bottom of the sea wall, chugging heartily off his forty ounce malt liquor bottle.

"Hieroglyphics, eh?" I repeated.

"There are guys at NASA that have hypothesized this, I'm not just making it up. Tatiana just confirmed it. This is not exactly classified stuff, but you're not supposed to know it. OK?"

"Sure, no problem."

"Tatiana said over one hundred people took to time-traveling long before it was proven safe. Apparently, these bracelets were inexpensive to make. Imagine the 3D printing they must have!

"Of that first group of explorers, or idiots, depends on who you ask, only ten have been tracked down. The rest, Tatiana said, were assumed to have arrived at places and times in history very hostile to human life. These devices were not exactly tuned to put you in a Paris coffee shop or Cleopatra's tent. You could have just as easily have ended up in a hungry bear's den or a velociraptor nest."

"Those ten that somehow survived…how? How do you know that?"

"There was an agreed pattern of symbols made among the group at that meeting. Whatever language they found themselves having to use, they were to leave a message, in script, hieroglyph, whatever, that would say, in this order: 'Hello from the children of Earth'.

"It was assumed that such a sequence of words would never occur to ancient peoples."

I looked at him with massive curiosity that must have made me look like a little kid.

"So, that phrase has been deciphered in ancient writings? Like you would find in an archaeological dig or something like that?"

"Yes. Ten times throughout history. Well up to present day. We even put it on the Voyager One spacecraft back in 1977. Just in case someone had managed to go forward in time."

I pondered all of this for a longer time than usual. Hudson, I knew, was quite comfortable not talking for a moment. He had just filled my head with a lot of things I was finding partially believable.

And, in my little slice of time, here on a large tropical mountain, mostly submerged in a large ocean, partially was enough for me.

Finally, I gathered my wits about me and thought again about what had prompted this discussion in the first place.

"So, Hudson, why did Tatiana give you your own bracelet? Are you supposed to follow her or go somewhere different? And, what the heck is she talking about when she says you invented this entire whatever, process. Time travel, Inter-Dimensional Shift. I don't know what to call it."

"No," he went to stand up.

I followed and climbed back down to the sidewalk.

"She warned me about putting it on. So I can only think it's a way for her to find me again."

We began walking back.

"As for inventing this whole mess, I'll have to defer to my future self. But, I suspect there's some secret in rainbows. Remember that idea you had once, about how light slows and bends, forming the colors?"

I remembered. If only I had been a mathematician, I might have proved the idea.

Hudson continued. "Like you said, the secret might be in how once those frequencies of light exit the water droplets, they reaccelerate to normal light speed. If you can hook up with that, you'll have a relativistic dilation of time."

I patted Hudson on the back. "Make it happen, bro."

~~~

There were a few early customers in the bar. Sandy and her trainee were easily keeping up. The stalk of green bananas at the end of the bar had not changed color for weeks now. I almost wondered if they had been picked so early they might never ripen.

I stopped a moment to chat with Sandy.

"So, how'd it go with Alana?"

"Oh, she made nice, but didn't say anything about wanting to come back to work." She looked at me with a touch of disappointment.

"Darn, I thought she would change her mind after she cooled off." I looked around and didn't see her.

"Did Alana leave already?"

Hudson stood next to me, listening as well.

"I guess so. She went out the back door."

Hudson and I quickly went into the hallway through the kitchen, passed my office and into the back where the hammock and car were. No Alana.

"Strange," Hudson said. "I would have thought she might hang around a little. You know."

Suddenly, I got a real bad feeling, turned and almost ran into my office. Hudson found me on the floor, slowly lifting up his empty backpack. All of the contents were strewn on the chair, on my desk, in the garbage can.

Hudson grabbed the backpack and went straight for the already opened side pocket. He thrust his hand inside, and for a moment, I thought he had found it there.

"Not good, bro. Not good," Hudson said, withdrawing his hand.

In it was the soft camera cloth and a handwritten note.

He read it and then handed the note to me, as I saw him slowly crouch down and sit on the floor. It said, "Aloha, Alana."

# LOST IN SPACE

The winding, two lane road that was the sole connection between forty thousand people on one side of Maui and the airport, hospital and big box stores was currently clogged with whale watching tourists. In their cars.

With every spout just offshore, the speeds decreased. We were currently moving along at a brisk eighteen miles per hour.

Usually, that's not a big problem. Take a deep breath and be thankful you aren't being nudged along at ninety on a Los Angeles freeway. But, today, I was driving Hudson to the airport to catch a chartered jet. One that would take him directly to Houston for a few days and then to Florida after that for a ride up to the Space Station.

At first, I had this obsession about being on time. Traffic wasn't helping my mood.

"They're not leaving without me," Hudson remarked. "We get there when we get there."

Now we were stopped for no apparent reason.

"I just want to go all Moses on this traffic and have it part right down the middle for me."

Hudson laughed, but being my brother he had to one up me.

"Yeah, well I bet Moses still got his feet muddy."

I turned to look at him, being conveniently stopped as we were.

"I like that," I said. "But, what does it mean?"

"It means," Hudson said. "That even when things go your way, there will probably still be some minor, but unpleasant consequences."

I'm sure we were both talking about Tatiana and Alana, but we would keep it a proxy discussion for now. Afterall, Hudson was back in the saddle again, and didn't need any bad mojo weighing on his mind.

That lasted about another thirty seconds.

"So, nothing on Alana?" Hudson asked.

I shook my head no.

"We filed a missing persons report three days after she stole your bracelet. Her last two paychecks have gone un-cashed. Her roommates and neighbors haven't seen her. Her bicycle is still out by the hammock."

Hudson nodded his head.

"Yeah, I guess she doesn't need any of those things now."

The traffic started to move again, but slowly.

"I wonder if she went back in time, or forward?"

Hudson seemed to know.

"Forward, to find Tatiana. That's what I'd guess. She's still addicted."

Another whale and a calf were rolling on their sides. Traffic stopped again.

"I'm glad you seemed able to kick that addiction. I guess it's just a trick of the ..."

"No," Hudson interrupted. "Tatiana did me two favors before she left. One was giving me the bracelet. The other was telling me how to kick the addiction. She said she had never told anyone how before."

"Really? How then?"

"She said Alana would show me. She did. As soon as we had sex, I felt the addiction fade."

"What?" I was flabbergasted. "Future Girl sure was a sex-obsessed one."

"Future Girl?"

"Yeah," I said. "That's my new name for Tatiana."

Hudson nodded with a smile. I could see this because we were stopped still. Unbelievable.

"I think what addiction I had transferred to Alana." Hudson sounded a little worried. "I tell you what bro, these girls from the future have mastered the art of manipulation."

"Ha! Imagine what the guys of the future are like!" I joked.

"There aren't many, at least according to Tatiana. They've got the genetic engineering so tricked out they simply don't reproduce the old-fashioned way. Tatiana said men, or the testosterone we carry around, had been the source of more war and suffering than anything else. They've practically eliminated the male half of the species."

A car horn behind me woke me from that bombshell. I let the car roll forward twenty feet and stopped again.

"Are you kidding me?"

"No. I think that's one reason why she liked me so much."

~~~

Ten days later Hudson was back in space. However, the two other cosmonauts that were to travel with him withdrew. Moscow said they had the flu, but offered no replacements. Washington sent Hudson by himself to save face.

The two guys that were already up there both came back on the RTE vehicle, despite Houston saying only one could. So, amazingly enough, Hudson was again by himself on the Space Station. Making matters worse was a deteriorating relationship between the Americans and Russians. No one had another rocket ready to take more crewmembers up. NASA told Hudson to expect a solitary mission of at least six months.

In an email Hudson said he was fine with it. He could catch up on his reading and tackle a few pet projects of his. Like the Unified Field Theory meets the Inter-Dimensional Shift for a game of Whose For Real?

Back at Tiwaka's Tiki Bar & Grill the world continued to spin at a predictable and comfortable rate. The clocks on the wall moved consistently forward, marching our lives from Winter to Spring to Fall and back again.

Tiwaka and the Waikikians were famous now, beyond our little Tiki bar, making international news. People anywhere near a coastline were trying to train birds to help their fishermen. I had to refuse multiple franchise requests from as far away as Thailand to the west and Sicily to the east.

Sandy and I were really making a go of it now. Working together in the Lahaina bar was fun. Baby Kiawe was growing up so fast that we played with the idea of having another. We played with that idea every night. God bless old-fashioned reproduction.

You can have the future!

~~~

One late night, right before my big stalk of green bananas began to finally ripen, someone claimed they had spotted Alana across the street. I immediately ran outside to check. Whoever they had seen wasn't there anymore.

I still wonder whatever happened to her. I suspect I'll never know.

The old cowboy that had complained about my green bananas hadn't been around in weeks. I asked around, because I had promised him the first ripe ones. No one had seen him.

So I invented a new kind of smoothie with just ripened bananas, vodka, rum, a variable amount of Tabasco and called it "Old Cowboy".

~~~

Hudson and I had been keeping in almost daily contact with email. I also had an app on my phone that told me when the Space Station would be passing over Maui. The six months since he had left had slipped by without any additional crew members launching. Only unmanned supply rockets.

Tonight, an hour after dark, my app said he'd be zipping overhead. We were going to try a Skype call, knowing it would probably only work for a minute or two.

Tiwaka sat on my shoulder as I took my smart(er than a parrot) phone outside, away from the noise of the bar. We walked over to a spot where the view of the sky was unobstructed by balconies or palm trees.

"I'm getting close," Hudson emailed.

"Standing by," I replied quickly. "But I think you need to initiate the call on your side."

"Will do," he replied.

"Will do," Tiwaka said, reading over my shoulder.

I turned to look at the parrot.

"Now you can read too?"

"Oui, mon ami."

A moment later the funny little Skype ringtone sounded and my app automatically launched. Tiwaka flapped his wings with excitement and I had to adjust my balance to compensate for the torque he generated.

"Hello from the children of Earth!" Hudson was laughing.

"Aloha bro!"

Tiwaka echoed me, perfectly.

Finally, the video came through. Hudson was gently floating in what appeared to be one of the recreation modules.

"I see you!" I said excitedly.

"Yeah, I see you and some ugly bird on your shoulder!"

Tiwaka squawked so loud I saw the video scramble for a moment.

"Just kidding, Tiwaka. You look fabulous!"

"So, howzit ..."

Hudson interrupted me quickly.

"Sorry, we've only got thirty seconds of video left. I've got to show you something."

I watched the video, with Tiwaka practically drooling over my shoulder. Hudson turned to look off camera, waving his hand.

"Look who's here!" Hudson said.

My jaw dropped as Tiwaka screamed out "Ooh La La!".

There, floating elegantly into view of the camera was a very happy Tatiana.

# ALOHA KAKOU

get the entire series!

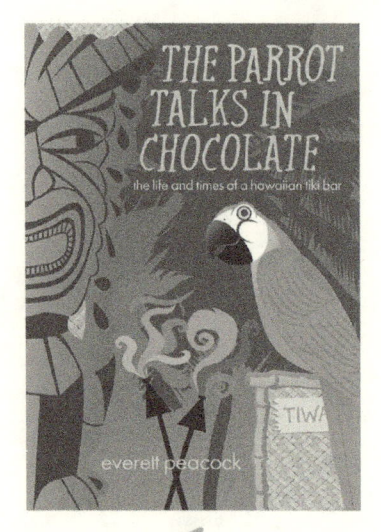

1. THE PARROT TALKS IN CHOCOLATE — the life and times of a hawaiian tiki bar — everett peacock

2. IN THE MIDDLE OF THE THIRD PLANET'S MOST WONDERFUL OF OCEANS — everett peacock

3. TIWAKA GOES TO WAIKIKI — EVERETT PEACOCK

4. GREEN BANANAS — EVERETT PEACOCK

## the playlist

### Ukulele Sunnyboy

Play the Game

Mountain Rag

On a Sunny Day

Dancing Waves

Summer Breeze

### DeVotchKa

The Winner Is

### Pearl Jam

Unthought Known

### Black Rebel Motocycle Club

Beat the Devil's Tattoo

### Matthew Peacock

theme song to "Whistle for My Horses"

Made in the USA
Coppell, TX
29 March 2025